Man's Man

BarbarianSpy

http://www.barbarianspy.com/

Man's Man

by habu

Table of Contents

Preface

Brian Hinton didn't set out to be a high-priced male prostitute based in L.A. but traveling far and wide to serve the desires and fetishes of rich and powerful men who could afford to pay $3,000 an hour for his attentions. Like many young, handsome men with acting talent that shines brightly on the small-town stage, Brian wanted to break into movie stardom. But also like many of these young men, he found that his greatest talent and charisma was in being at the beck and call of already-successful men with unusual appetites and thick wallets.

Unlike some of these other men, though, Brian embraced the possibilities and made the most of the natural allure that he evoked in other man and, with gusto and without apologies or reservations, entered into a fascinating life of making the most of what he had in a reality-based arc in the spotlight that, in this collection of stories of sexual gay male encounter begins in naïve, overstretching ambition and ends with a satisfied sigh.

Chapter 1: Slippery Slope

I hadn't given any thought really to how I was going to lose my virginity before I did so. But then I was so narcissistic in those days that I didn't give much thought at all to anything but what a handsome and talented fellow I was. It helped that I was, in fact, very well built and endowed and was good at everything I tried and had no lack of offers to lose my virginity early.

I was the best thing on two legs the year I graduated from high school. Star quarterback of the football team, lead in the senior play, king of the prom, and I was the lead singer for a rock band that was well-known and highly appreciated for a good hundred yards beyond all borders of my high school district. I could have collected cherries left and right, I'm sure, if I wasn't more stuck on myself than any of my classmates were on me. I wouldn't have noticed a pass or an offer for sex in those days if it were engraved on my forehead. The yearbook predicted I would be a movie star—and I, of course, believed what my yearbook said.

Being a movie star was exactly what I wanted to be. I won best leading actor in the statewide North Carolina high school tournament play competitions my senior year, which included a pretty good scholarship to the drama department at

UNC. But I didn't have time to go the slow route, and, besides, I was so good I didn't need more drama or music—or even dance—training. I was a star—at least in the Lee-Jackson High School district not too far out of Winston-Salem, North Carolina. My parents really did want me to go to college before striking out for Hollywood—although to their credit they never did anything to discourage my interest in acting—and I might have been convinced to at least start at UNC on that scholarship if it hadn't been for Martin Blixen. Blixen had been a Broadway play director and was still putting on productions on Off Broadway in New York. He had been the head judge at the North Carolina play tournament and had taken me aside and told me that I was the greatest natural actor he'd seen in many years. And he offered me a spot in the summer stock cast he was putting together for the Barter Theater in the southern Virginia town of Abingdon for that summer.

UNC told me I could put taking up my scholarship on hold for a year as long as I was still working in drama—that I could even tally up some credits by working for pay in summer stock—so the decision to take off for Abingdon was sort of a no-brainer. Blixen said he needed me to play the young hunk in his summer production of Ira Levin's *Deathtrap*, and I couldn't very well start off on a career in the theater by pissing off a big-time New York stage director.

Blixen was really nice and attentive to me in the rehearsals for the play, which was about Sidney Bruhl, a has-been playwright, who decides to steal a blockbuster script from his protégé, Clifford, and reclaim his fame by calling it his own. The only problem is that he has to figure out a way to get rid of Clifford in the process. I was playing the mid-twenties Clifford, and a thirty-something actor from Blixen's Off Broadway troupe was being made up to look a distinguished fifty to play Sidney.

Hunter Elliott, which, of course, was a stage name, who was playing Sidney, was a terrific help to me. He took me under his wing and taught me so much about stagecraft that I had no idea even existed. And he was very attentive both as an older actor helping a younger one and in his stage role, because Blixen was bending the play script to give a hint of something sexual between the older playwright and his protégé.

I didn't even see it coming. I was so much taken with myself and the seriousness of the stage career that I was so easily seizing that I just thought that Hunter Elliott was a terrific character actor.

We had quite a suggestive scene on stage, where we actually kissed. I was embarrassed, of course, but Hunter was so good at making me comfortable that I was completely focused on myself and how I would be coming across to the audience that I assumed that Hunter was just acting.

The opening night went extremely well, and I was ecstatic at the applause I had gotten. I was walking on air when we returned to our rooms in a wing off of the Barter Theater, where the summer stock cast lived during the season. Hunter and I were sharing a room—and a bath. We had all of that yucky stage makeup on and it had run terribly under the stage lights, so neither of us could wait to hit the shower when we finally broke away from all of the smiling well-wishers who had descended on the dressing room after the performance. The main problem is that we only had one shower stall.

"You can shower first," I said as we came through the door of our room.

"We could, of course, shower together," Hunter said. "You know, to celebrate our huge opening night." Then he laughed lightly when I didn't react—react either way really.

"Did you hear them applaud when I left the stage after the opening scene of act two, Hunter?" I asked. "They got it; they got what I was working to convey to them."

"Yes, right," Hunter muttered. "You were great. The audience couldn't get enough of you. And I'd like to get some of that too." He started stripping off his clothes.

"Think I can get Martin to move me farther downstage, right up to the footlights, for the recognition scene?" I asked.

"I'm sure Blixen would let you stand anywhere you wanted, as long as you let him do you," Hunter said. "Which brings us to . . ."

"That'd be great if he did that," I said. And, of course, I wasn't listening to a thing Hunter Elliott was saying.

11

"Me first in the shower and then us," Hunter said brightly. "OK?"

"Ummmm," was my unresponsive response. "A brighter light too. The audience could hang on every nuance of the change in my expression."

Elliott was gone into the bathroom, and I kept musing aloud. This was the biggest opening night of my life. "This was the biggest opening night of my life," I called out to the bathroom, sure that Hunter was reveling in my stage initiation as much as I was.

Elliott, however, was intent on another form of initiation. "Yep, we're gonna get you opened big tonight," he called back.

It was a loud stream of water coming out of the shower, though, and I wasn't paying a bit of attention to whatever words Elliott was saying that didn't include praise for my opening night performance.

I didn't even half process how aroused he was when he came out of the bathroom, naked and at half mast already.

While he was showering, I'd stripped down. "My turn?" I asked as I brushed past him and into the bathroom.

"Yep, this is where you get yours, good buddy," Elliott said with a big, sloppy grin on his face.

On any other night but my first paid opening stage night, I probably would have processed what Hunter Elliott was up to when he came back into the bathroom wearing only a condom. But this was my "it's all about me" stage of my life, and I'd just had the most acclaim and emotional stroking of my life.

Elliott at least had the good grace to start off with some "pretend" reason for being naked in the shower with me.

"Back massage," He said, just loudly enough through the hiss of the shower for it to register as a reasonable event. "I think I've mentioned that it's really important to massage those muscles after a performance—or you'll be too tight and will cramp on stage during the next performance."

"Hunter . . . ," I started. Knowing there was something "not right" about this, but too euphoric to focus on what it was.

"Turn around, hands on wall, lean in," Elliott commanded. And I complied.

Elliott actually did give the greatest massage that released the tension and that went pretty far toward releasing the inhibitions as well. It wasn't like I didn't think Hunter was attractive and hadn't felt close and grateful to him for all the help and attention he'd been giving me. I didn't want him to stop once he had started, and he obviously didn't want to stop either. And when he got his hands down to my buns and started rolling them and separating them and running his thumbs across my channel entrance, I merely grunted and murmured that he should stop. My requests for him to stop pushing his thumbs inside my entrance were also weakened by how arousing his massage was—and they were ignored anyway.

By the time he was crouched behind me and separating my butt cheeks and going at my hole with his tongue, I didn't really care all that much what he wanted to do. I liked being loved. The adoration I'd felt coming at me from across the footlights was intoxicating; what Hunter was doing was just an extension of that. Giving me the adoration I deserved on a night of triumph. And besides, I was more aroused than I'd ever been before and I rather thought I'd like to stay aroused.

When he decided I was open enough for him, he stood up, close behind me, and brought his strong arms around and massaged my arm and torso and thigh muscles as I felt his engorged cock rubbing up and down in the small of my back. Then he was kissing the hollow of my neck and massaging the muscle between my legs and his hard cock had been pushed down between my crack . . . and at last found purchase at my entrance. And then he was slowly entering me while I grunted and groaned and objected in jerky exclamations of mixed pain and pleasure in a weak, unconvincing voice. I writhed within his strong grip under the running shower and cried out at the loss of my virginity as his throbbing cock slowly stretched me and started the first journey of my experience in having a strong cock fuck up into me.

He had my face turned to his and was giving me a far

more intimate kiss than we performed on stage, when I went over the edge at the first stroking of my cock by the hand of another man and spouted my semen against the slick tile wall of the shower stall.

When the frenzied taking had ended, I broke away in shock and embarrassment and shame and ran out of the bathroom. I barely had the chance to pull on my jeans before fleeing the room in search of . . . in search of . . . I wasn't sure what I searching for. I had no one to blame but myself. I hadn't exactly resisted it.

Instinctively I headed for the stage area of the theater. Some of the stage lights were still on and I heard movement back in the dressing room area.

Martin Blixen was still there, in the men's dressing room, making sure the costumes had been put back where they belonged—ready for the next evening's performance.

"What's happened, Brian? You look . . . ," Blixen blurted as he saw me standing, shivering, in the dressing room door despite the 90-degree heat.

"Hunter . . . Hunter," I managed to say through a moan. "He's . . . in the shower . . . I . . . we . . ."

"Hunter fucked you?" Blixen cried out, his voice full of rage. He evidently knew just by seeing me what had happened.

"God . . . oh, oh . . . yes, he . . ."

"That bastard," Blixen mutter again. "He knows . . . Here, son, come here. It will be all right."

And I stumbled over to him and we both sank down on the edge of a daybed. He enveloped me in his arms and rocked me back and forth and whispered to me about how everything would be all right. He was running his hands through my hair, and I felt his lips at my cheek, under my ear lobe, as he whispered assurances at me.

I heard and felt my jeans being unzipped as he rocked me back and forth, but I didn't care. He was being very comforting. He had been so fathering during the whole rehearsal process. And he thought I was a great actor. He had told me so. He had told me that he'd help me get my break in Hollywood.

I was fully aware now what he was going to do to me— and it was no different really than what I'd just allowed Hunter to do with me. The difference was that Blixen could further my career—if I pleased him. If I could endure what was going to happen, what he wanted from me. And I'd just endured it from Elliott. It wasn't like I had anything to protect any more.

He knelt between my legs and pulled my jeans off as he took my cock inside his mouth and sucked me until I was sighing and groaning and had released my seed down his throat. Then he was sitting on the daybed beside me again and had pulled me up into his lap and slowly skewered my ass on his hard cock, with me spreading my legs as much as possible and arching my shoulder blades into his chest, trying to open to him as painlessly as possible. And then we were rocking back and forth, him still humming and singing softly to me, as he fucked me and fucked me and fucked me. When he felt me shaking and ready to collapse after being pumped up and down in his lap, he turned me on my side on the daybed and laid stretched behind me, lifted my leg in the air, and thrust impatiently up into my channel, as I howled to the corner of the room.

I was still gasping and hiccupping between low sobs when Blixen had come inside me and gently pulled out from behind me and let me curl up in a fetal position on the daybed beside him.

"What do I do now?" I whined between sobs.

"You just go on," Blixen said. He was running his hands along the contours of my body, registering every nook and cranny of me, and I could tell from his humming that he was enjoying his exploration. A hand came around and cupped my balls and squeezed and pulled them away from my body, and I moaned for him. "It was past time that you had this happen to you. It will make you a stronger actor. It's all good experience. Your work in this play will be even better now."

I sobbed on briefly. "But where can I go now?"

"Back to your room. You're a man now. A man's man, just like so many of the actors you will encounter. You will never be without an opportunity to fuck or be fucked in this

15

business—not as long as your keep your looks and you natural presence—that charisma you have that makes a man's cock harden as you walk into the room. This was inevitable. I saw that you were responsive when Hunter kissed you onstage. I knew it would only be a matter of time." And then much more quietly, as if I wasn't expected to hear it. "But damn that bastard, Hunter. He knew . . ."

"But Hunter will be there."

"Just give him the cold shoulder," Blixen said. "You're a great actor. Even if it has made you distraught—which is really a little precious for an actor, you know. Show him distain. That will make his cock go limp. You should have experienced fucking a long time before now—don't let him know it bothers you. And don't let him touch you again."

But it wasn't as easy as Blixen seemed to think. I did go back to my room, but I wasn't there more than three minutes before I was flat on my back on my bed with Hunter crouched and grunting between my spread legs and fucking me in long, deep strokes. My eyes were pretty much opened now to the added duties of my summer stock experience.

"Bet he was mad at me," Hunter said with a belabored grunt. "You know he wanted you first, don't you?"

"Oh, God, Hunter. Slower, please. Don't . . . oh, shit Yessssss! Do that again."

"Bet he told you not to let me have you again, didn't he? He does this every year. Brings in some young hunk and smothers him with praise—all to get his dick dipped. You were the best of the lot, though, so I decided to do you first. He won't do anything to me. I'm doing him, you know."

No, I didn't know. But I was learning pretty fast. It would take more than this to turn me from my grab at Hollywood, though. Much more. Blixen was right. The first time had to come at some time or another—and much of my embarrassment was that I was not sexually seasoned before I came to work under him. Best not to mourn what couldn't be restored.

Chapter 2: Use It

"You . . . got . . . that 'It factor,' Brian. Use it and you'll . . . ahhhhhh . . . go far."

I had to admire Hunter Elliott. He could continue to give me instruction, even when I was sitting in his lap and pumping myself hard on his engorged cock. As for myself, there was no way I could do more than moan and grunt as he gave me a fast-track primer on pleasing a top.

"Now for what I call the Dying Swan maneuver," Hunter directed. "Oh, yes, baby . . . just like that. I can get in soooo deep. Ahhhhh."

He was sitting on the edge of my bed in our shared room in the actor's quarters at the summer stock Barter Theater in southern Virginia, and I was facing him, my knees on either side of his thighs and lapped on his throbbing tool. At his direction, I arched back until my shoulder blades rested on his shin bones, and I undulated my pelvis, taking him deep inside me.

"Oh, yes, baby. The directors out in Hollywood are going to love you. You're good on the stage. But not so much better than lots of other honey-tongued southern hunks. Where you'll shine is in the bedroom, if you just learn how to use what you've got. Now we do the Jackhammer."

17

And, with that, the somewhat older, but appreciably more accomplished actor who was playing the other male part in our run of *Deathtrap* continued broadening my education. He had been my first, no more than three weeks earlier, so this was definitely a crash course.

"Oh, god," I cried out, as Hunter rose up on his feet, pushing my shoulder blades down to the floor, grabbed my thighs to hold me in place, and started thrusting his cock hard down into me.

Hunter was a good teacher, and he imparted a lot of useful information with his fucking, but I probably wouldn't have shed my inhibitions so totally after a lifetime of cluelessness and begun to learn how to really use my body to my best advantage if it hadn't been the night courses I was receiving from the play's director, the once-well-known stage director, Martin Blixen, who now was fitting summer stock productions in with Off-Broadway theater.

That same night, after Hunter and I had showered off our stage makeup from another well-received performance of *Deathtrap* and he'd fucked me in the shower, I went, as summoned, to the room of Martin Blixen. He was naked and ready for me, and, at his instruction, I gave him prolonged and deep head, kneeling on my knees between his spread thighs.

Blixen wasn't the inventive acrobat that Hunter was, nor did he have as much stamina. But he was better endowed than Hunter was and taxed my channel muscles and made me cry out in passion and overtaxing filling as Hunter never quite achieved.

We were stretched out on his bed on our sides, Blixen behind me, with his cock side-splitting me deep and relentlessly in long, powerful strokes, while he worried one of my nipples with pinching fingers and kissed me in the hollow of my neck. I was arching back to him and panting hard and groaning at his master cocking of me.

"What is it, son?" he whispered in my ear. "I know there's something on your mind. Tell Daddy. Oh . . . yes, yes. Work those channel muscles on my cock. You are so good. Such a natural. Tell Daddy. Whatever you want that I can give you. Yesssss!"

"The running of the play ends in a couple of weeks," I murmured to him. "And there isn't a part for me in the one that follows, is there?"

"That's right," he answered. "But you have no fears if you want to stay on. You can be my assistant. You enjoy working under me, don't you?"

He pulled my thigh back, pulling my ass back harder onto his plundering cock.

"Ahhhhhh," I cried out. "Yes, yes, I enjoy working under you. . . . But I want to get out to Hollywood. Do you know anyone out there . . . directors, producers . . . anyone you can write a recommendation to for me?"

Hunter would be proud of me. I was already using "it."

* * * *

It was also thanks to Hunter that I made my next move.

"The Chrysler Players in Norfolk need a 'hunk' actor for their fall season . . . and you can make much more on top of that in half the time as a dancer at the Bad Boys' Den there near the naval base," he'd told me when I had the letter I wanted from Blixen in hand. "Not in dancing, of course, but in quick tricks. You'll need money to last for a good six months if you really want a chance of making it in Hollywood."

"Thanks Hunter," I answered. "But I wished there was another way."

"What did I tell you about needing to use it?" he asked.

He'd just shown me how strong his leg muscles were, having made me climb up onto his hips in the shower while he pushed my back up and down the slicked shower tiles with the strength of his thigh muscles and his hard cock. We were laying on the bed, entwined and exploring each other with wandering hands.

"Yeah, I guess," I said. But I still wished there was another way. "The letter Blixen gave me is to some dude named Rex Reeson," I said. "I've never heard of him, but Blixen said he's a major producer out there and can really fix me up."

"He's sending you to Reeson?" Hunter asked. And I could feel the tension in his voice permeating throughout his body.

"Yeah, is there something wrong with that?" I asked.

There was a long pause. "No, I guess not," Hunter said with a sigh. "Blixen is usually a good judge of these things. I guess Reeson might be the right one for you. But for now, more instruction. I'm now going to show you the Reverse Thrust."

And he did. And I was sore for hours afterward from it.

* * * *

The Chrysler Players were a pretty long step down from the Barter Theater, but they paid enough to cover my room and board, and, with Hunter Elliott's recommendations, the gig at the Bad Boys' Den gave me a good start on accumulating a nest egg for a run at Hollywood.

The dance club was a form of Chippendale's for men. For the first couple of months, it wasn't bad at all. I'd get some base money from the club for dancing and then a couple times more than that in my G-string from mostly middle-aged men with unfulfilled fantasies. When I'd learned to let the G-string accidentally slip off three quarters of the way through my set, I doubled my income along with coming a lot closer to fulfilling some fantasies.

Not all of the men were failing to fulfill their fantasies, of course. The Bad Boys' Den had a couple of backstage cubicles with cots, and if I let just two or three of the patrons go back there with me in an evening, I could add $100 to my stash. $25 for a blow job, either given or received, and $50 for a quick doggy fuck.

This wasn't anywhere close to what my dream of a Hollywood career had looked like back when I was the toast of my small town in North Carolina, but I was slowly building up that nest egg. One of the best lessons Hunter Elliott had taught me was not to take Hollywood on without at least six months of living money—and finding out what constituted living money on the California coast was a real eye opener.

Still, as steadily as I was saving, I'd probably still be doing quick fucks in Norfolk if tragedy hadn't struck when the fleet came in from maneuvers in early November.

I had known that the Bad Boys' Den was on the far edge of the red-light district devoted to the Norfolk naval base, but until those randy sailors got their shore leaves from the fall maneuvers out in the Atlantic off Hampton Roads, I had had no idea what really kept the dancehall afloat.

On the first evening of the shore leaves, the sailors descended on us in virtual waves of raunchy-voiced, grabby-hands humanity. Most of the seasoned dancers managed not to be scheduled that first night. They wanted their share of the Navy's money, certainly, but they knew to get it on the third or fourth night when the sailors had calmed down and the rowdiest of them had been thrown in the brig by the shore patrol. Only neophytes like me didn't scheme to avoid that first night.

The first couple of hours of my shift went fine, and I pulled in a good $500, mostly in money patted into my waistband while the benefactor was copping a good feel. And I made four trips back to one of the cubicles and could have made more trips if the cubicles weren't in such high demand. The sailors, who had been at sea for a couple of months right up until this first shore leave day, weren't interested in blow jobs. They all wanted a good piece of my ass.

It was at the end of my shift that tragedy struck. When my replacement came in, I somewhat reluctantly changed into a T and my jeans, rolled up my wad of newly earned Hollywood-bound money, and left by the stage door into the dark alley. I was so preoccupied with mourning the money that I could have made if I'd stayed that the three bulky sailors lurking in the shadows there had me subdued and pulled back behind a row of trash barrels before I knew what was happening.

I initially tried to fight them off, but they pounded me down and let me know that I'd be beaten to a pulp if I didn't give them what they wanted.

What they wanted was to fuck me. Each of them, in succession, and brutally. One held me from behind in a full Nelson, while one of the others pulled my jeans off and spread my legs and held my thighs in strong, calloused hands as he pounded my ass with a dick that hadn't been dipped in months. Then, when he was ready to come, he dropped my legs, pulled his dick out of me, and pushed my face down to receive the full force of his ejaculation. While he was spouting off, the one behind me thrust his dick between my butt cheeks from behind and doggy fucked me. The third sailor laid me on my back on top of a low, closed barrel, and his buddies helped to hold me down and keep my legs spread as he fucked me missionary style.

Worse than wanting unpaid sex, they also wanted my bankroll from the evening, and they just took it after punching me down a couple of more times so I didn't feel like coming after them when they left the alley.

I wasn't in any condition to be working for the rest of the shore leave period, so I lost out completely on the main business of the Bad Boys' Den.

That was too rough for me. But when I told the dancehall owner I was quitting, he begged me to stay, saying I was one of the club's main draws. When that didn't work out, though, he revealed that he had something of an escort service running on the side and did I want to move on to that?

When I saw what that entailed and what I could make, I said, "Sure." I also easily saw why he kept the service a secret from his dancers. I figured I could make twice the money as essentially a one-on-one callboy as I could dancing and with, arguably, half the effort.

At Christmas time, I hit pay dirt.

The boy toy of the owner of a major seashore resort on Virginia's Eastern Shore, across the Chesapeake Bay Bridge-Tunnel from Norfolk, decided to give his "daddy" a bit of variety as his Christmas present. Through the escort service, I was engaged to take a day's boat ride with the two of them out into the Chesapeake Bay.

The resort owner, who was introduced to me as Howard Stidwell but whose name quickly drifted into the back of my mind, looked good for a man in his fifties. He'd taken good care of himself and from the way he moved around the yacht we went out on, I could see that he'd never been afraid of doing honest, strenuous work. He had a good, strong build, and a nice mane of silver hair. He'd look good on TV lying to people convincingly on why his company executives lived in mansions and his line employees were on food stamps.

The boy toy was somewhat of a clone of me. Very good looking, well muscled, graceful in his movements, and with a extra big cock. We weren't alone, though. The yacht came with a one-man crew, a chocolate-skinned hunk with honestly earned ropy musculature and a big, friendly smile.

For the first part of the afternoon, the Christmas present boy only wanted to watch me and his boy toy, both stripped down and taking a tan on a hatch at the bow of the yacht.

As the afternoon wore on, though, and even though the resort owner still wanted to watch, he had moved to wanting to watch his boy toy fuck me, with me stretched out on my belly on the hatch and the boy toy stretched full length over me and fucking down into my ass with a really nice cock.

After that, the resort owner wanted to watch the chocolate-brown crew hulk fuck me on the cushions of the bench running around the fantail of the yacht. I particularly enjoyed that, as the hulk enjoyed the opportunity to participate, handled me quite expertly, and laughed with good humor as he fucked.

After a dinner of fresh-caught and boiled lobster while we floated out on the Chesapeake Bay in the waning light of the day, the resort owner had finished watching. He took me to his cabin and bounced me around on the walls for hours, fucking me in uncountable positions and three ways from Sunday and showing remarkable staying and recuperative powers for a man his age. Up to that time, I had thought the boy toy had an easy and probably quite boring life, but that one night was enough to show me that he really earned his keep and had probably

23

thought of this present idea to get a night off.

I earned $500 for that one night. And I laughed in later years when I thought back to this time and remembered how I thought I had found the mother lode with that single assignment.

I must have given the resort owner full satisfaction, because only a couple of days after New Years, my services were leased to him full time. I moved in with him in his penthouse apartment at the seaside resort. There was no sign of his boy toy, so I understood that this function was now mine. He fucked me every night and almost endlessly into the spring, when I had earned enough money to try out Hollywood. I had certainly used all of the resources I could muster, but I had not lost sight of my goal. The resort owner was sorry to see me go, or so the expression on his face and the tenderness of his last fuck told me, but we parted on good terms, with him saying I could always return to him if I needed to and my leaving with a $1,000 in bonus money.

I turned my face to the west and locked my eyes on Hollywood.

Chapter 3: Twice Taken

Within a week of getting out to the West Coast and settling in a small apartment, I presented myself at the Los Angeles offices of the producer, Rex Reeson; hand delivered my letter of recommendation from the Off-Broadway director I'd worked for and been bedded by, Martin Blixen; and requested an appointment. The thirty-something carbon copy of so many "recently were" pretty-boy beach muscle guys who introduced himself as Reeson's West Coast personal assistant ushered me into his office and gave me a big smile of welcome. I kept the letter shoved under his nose, one of three certified copies I'd had made in case I needed to use it more than once.

"Yes, yes, I'm sure Mr. Reeson would like to help you, Mr. Hinton. Or may I call you Brian? Yes, thanks, Brian. But Mr. Reeson is in France now. The Cannes festival and then some interviewing of young French men. I don't expect him back for two months or more." The smooth talker couldn't have been more concerned and contrite, but that didn't help me much.

"I do need to see him as soon as possible," I said. "Mr. Blixen told me he would be sure—"

"Yes, yes, if Martin Blixen has recommended you, I'm sure we can do something for you. But Mr. Reeson simply isn't here."

My dejection was palpable, I'm sure. I couldn't just wait around doing nothing. "But, while you are waiting, I guess I could arrange an interview for something that would help tide you over. How does that sound?"

I perked up immediately. "Yes, that would be great, Mr. . . ."

"You can just call me Leon," he answered. "Of course, you may not want to try it. It's all I can offer at the moment, though, and I couldn't make any promises beyond that. Mr. Reeson . . . well, I think you can understand."

"Yes, I'm sure. What sort of production is it?"

"Well, it's an art film . . . of men . . . for men," Leon answered. And he had his eyes plastered on my face, looking for how this set with me.

Oh. And my balloon burst. But only the one on the inside. I used all of my acting ability to hold myself together on the outside. I needed some sort of job, some income. My nest egg was already hemorrhaging at an alarming rate. My research on California had been laughable; I had been shocked at the notion of how much living on the West Coast would cost me. But I had seriously underestimated what it would really cost me.

"Yes, of course I'll give it a try," I answered.

Leon beamed a smile of approval at me.

* * * *

"So, you are here to audition for my movies," Mr. S said to me as I entered the living room to the hotel suite. He was the director of Ruby Bulb films, and, even with the introduction from Rex Reeson's West Coast personal assistant, Leon, I'd been waiting for two weeks to see him, as he only gave two auditions a day. I could tell which one was the big director immediately when I came into the room, as he was a Big Daddy Warbucks type, all height and big bones and muscles, and no hair. Two other two men in the room were holding movie cameras and were looking a little disheveled and disinterested. The third man, sitting quietly over in a corner,

26

came as a complete surprise—Reeson's personal assistant, Leon.

Mr. S was all smiles and hearty handshakes and shoulder pats, the type of man who made you keep your hand on your wallet whenever you were within ten feet of him. I answered that, indeed, I was here to audition for his movies.

"And you know these are gay art films, don't you?" he continued. "There's a ton of money for actors to make in these films. They can lead to the big movie world. Why, did you know . . . ," and he was reeling off the names of several name-brand actors who had started in this segment of the industry only to rise to the big screen—some of the most macho actors of the day.

I wagged my head agreeably, trying to keep up with him and present him my best profile all at the same time.

"Well, we might as well get started," Mr. S said with a laugh. "There are two other interviews for this part pushing in on the day's schedule. Leon over there pressed me hard to fit you in. Put those application forms over on that desk and strip down over there and then come back over here."

"Strip? Here, now?" I stammered.

"This is the audition, son. You did say that you understood that these were gay porn films? You can't audition in your clothes. I can't make any decisions if I don't see the goods. Don't worry, this should only take fifteen or twenty minutes. We'll have to put an audition scene on tape so that I have something to work with when I'm casting."

I looked a little dubious and not just a little embarrassed. He was right, though. What had I thought would go into an audition for male porn films? I went over and put my carefully prepared application forms down on the desk and started to strip, neatly folding my clothes on the desk chair.

"Oh, and there's a release form for you to sign for the screen test tape there on the desk," Mr. S said, as he walked over to a sofa. "You'll even be paid $50 just for being permitted to try out and being put on film."

When I had stripped, I turned and walked toward Mr. S, who was standing in front of the sofa. He'd stripped down to his jockey shorts.

"You?" I said, a big lump forming in my throat. "I'll be auditioning with you?"

"Yes, of course," Mr. S answered. "I like to know exactly what my actors can and cannot do. Oh, and call me Rolf. We're going to get to know each other much too well for formalities."

Why should I be surprised, I thought. Tales of the casting couch were legendary in—and about—this town.

"Well, aren't you the nice looker?" Rolf said to me as I came closer to the sofa. "Turn around for me. Ah yes, very presentable. The boy next door look. The athletic boy next door look. The horse-hung boy next door look. But with something special, something that men will naturally gravitate to. I suppose that's why Leon sent you to us."

"I suppose," I said, very embarrassed at Rolf's straightforwardness, and a little muddled, as Leon had no knowledge of what I was packing or how I looked naked—at least until now. Now he was leaning forward in his chair, very much interested in what he was seeing.

"Come, come," Rolf said and gestured his hand at me. I moved closer to him, and he kneaded and prodded me like I was some sort of stud horse he was contemplating buying, which, I guess, I pretty much was auditioning to be. He turned me this way and that way and ran his hands over my torso, arms, and legs. He handled my cock and balls like they were a purse and shoes set he was considering, and then he patted me on the buttocks and sat down in front of me.

"Stroke your cock to hard for me, please, Brian. The cocks are the real stars of our little movies. Ahh, yes, very nice. Very nice indeed. You are a big boy, aren't you?"

I assumed that was a rhetorical question and didn't require answering. This new experience was making me tense, and I was really afraid I'd come here in front of Mr. S and his camera crew. That would really be a problem, as I knew porn actors were supposed to have extraordinary holding power. Little did I know then that what looked like one scene was several takes and several repeats of film footage.

"Now, we will be running through this screen test fairly quickly, Brian," Mr. S was saying. "There are a certain number of things I have to check out. During the audition, I will be directing in a low voice what you are to do and what emotions you are to project. Do you understand that? And how well and quickly—and without hesitation—you follow my directions will have everything to do with your audition success. You are to pay no attention to the cameras or to the boom mike when it comes down to pick up the dialogue, of which there will be practically none. Do you understand? Good. Lights and roll 'em."

The room was suddenly flooded with strong lighting.

"I'm going to kiss you first, and you are to be surprised initially and then to surrender to me."

He pulled me into his body brutally and took my mouth with his. We kissed deeply, with me slowly warming to him. When he broke away, he was smiling. "Very nice kisser," he whispered to me.

Then Rolf sat on the sofa in front of me, took me by the hips, and pulled me toward his head.

"Now, I am going to suck you off. I will do so rather quickly," he whispered to me. "You are to look surprised and to contemplate trying to push me off but come to love what I'm doing." And, with that, he pulled my hips into his face and drew my cock into his mouth. I arched my back away from him, trying to make it seem that I was going to attempt to move out of his clutches. Then I put my hands on his bald head and acted like I was trying to push him away. I tried to convey fear, uncertainty, and unwillingness in my facial expressions. Rolf had his hands dug into my butt cheeks, holding me there, and the camera men moved in and out around us, creating and milking their shots.

I slowly changed my facial expressions to acceptance and then to desire. I moved my hands to the back of his head, cupping him into me rather than trying to push him away. And I started to move my hips with the motions of the pumping of his mouth muscles. It wasn't all acting. Rolf really knew how to give head. The boom mike came down to pick up my light moaning and sighing. I felt one of his hands leave a butt cheek and move in between my legs and under my balls, and the fingers glide up to my asshole. He slowly inserted a finger inside me. It was pushing its way up my chute and stopped, finger pad on prostate.

Rolf took his mouth from my cock and instructed me sotto voce, "I'm going to make you come now. I will release your cock just before you come, and then I want you to shoot off on my chest. I will force you down to lick that off and then I will force you to suck me off. Again, you should show some form of unwillingness to do this, but not enough to prevent it from happening or for us not to be able to say it was just shy reluctance."

I wondered how Rolf would make me come on cue, but his finger on my prostate seemed to have that part fully under control. I shot off on his chest and then struggled a bit with him as he forced me to my knees between his legs and my head down to his chest. His chest was as hairless as the rest of him, and his pecs and nipples were massive. He had an elaborate starburst tattooed around one nipple that intrigued me greatly. I licked the saltiness of me off his chest and then struggled with him as he pushed his briefs down and off his legs and forced my face down to a cock that was even thicker than mine, although not nearly as long. It made me gasp, though, as it was crowned with a huge, bulbous, dark-red head.

"Like it?" Rolf whispered. "Hence the name for my movie company. Meet and greet the ruby bulb." Then, after giving a lusty laugh, he took my head in both hands and forced my lips down hard on his cock, pushing it in and making me gag and gurgle. I didn't have to act out the assault nature of this grinding of cock into face for the cameras at all. He laced his legs around my calves, holding me to him, and held one of my arms by the wrist, while burying the fingers of his other hand in the hair at the back of my head and moving my head back and forth in rhythm to the pumping of his prick in my mouth.

After just a few minutes of this, he brought his lips down to my ears and whispered, "Now, I'm going to backhand you with a stage slap and send you spinning to the corner of the sofa next to me, while I roll a condom on and come up with a tube of lubricant. And then I'm going to set you on my lap and you are going to struggle until I'm inside you and then you are gradually going to surrender to me. And then the screen test will end. Understand?"

I nodded for him.

Rolf raised me up, snapping my head off his dick, and backhanded me strongly across the mouth, which, indeed made me spin naturally and breathlessly onto my back on the sofa beside him. If this was supposed to have been a stage slap, I certainly had no idea how those were supposed to be done. It certainly wasn't the simulated action I had been trained to do on stage. Genuinely stunned, I lay there while Rolf pulled a condom packet and a tube of lube from under the sofa cushion and rolled the condom onto his dick.

I was only half acting that I was struggling with him, as he turned and grabbed me by the biceps with strong hands and pulled me onto his lap, facing him. I was doing what I could to stay off his cock by crouching on the sofa cushions with my knees on either side of his hips. I was pushing at his pecs with my fists, arching my back away from him, and giving my best "this isn't my idea of fun" expression for the cameras, which were buzzing around us and shooting the action from all angles.

Rolf got a gob of lubricant on the fingers of one hand and was fingering my asshole, lubing me up, while his other hand grabbed me here and there, keeping me on his lap. And then with one camera rolling up close from the front and the other one from the back, he grabbed me around the waist and pulled me down onto Ruby Bulb and slowly down until the curls of down on my butt cheeks met his hairless groin.

The boom mike came down to catch my cries and grunts and groans, which followed Rolf's directions nicely, but would not have changed regardless of what he had told me he wanted me to do. My body trembled, and I arched my back and screwed up my eyes tight, as he was skewering me. But as I accommodated to him—and remembered his directions—I

31

slowly let the tension drain from my body. His pelvis was undulating, letting Ruby Bulb rub around my ass canal walls deep. I let my fists open on his pecs and cup them, my palms covering his nipples. And I let my eyes meet his, and the cameras watch the desire that we both could express with our eyes. I leaned down into him, our lips meeting in a long, lingering kiss. Then I started a rhythm with my own hips, stroking his cock up and down inside of me.

Rolf rose from the sofa and turned me to where I was laying back on the sofa and he was crouched above me. He wishboned my legs and churned back and forth inside me with his thick cock in long strokes. The camera buzzed around and the boom mike came down to pick up my pants and moans.

Rolf quickly got tired of this position. He pulled out of me and stretched me out on my belly on the sofa and then straddled my hips with his knees and pumped me from above in long strokes. I heard him give a little cry, and he pulled out of me and showed the cameras that he was a virile man and that this was a real fuck shoot by quickly peeling off the condom and spouting out across my back. As he lowered his chest on my back, he huskily yelled "Cut!" and the strong lights died.

As I was dressing, I got up the nerve to ask him about the audition. "So, how was I?" I asked with a stammer in my voice.

"You were great, kid," Rolf answered jovially. "Leon was right in sending you to us. You're made to be a star in this business."

"So, do I stand a chance to be in your film?" I pressed.

"Damn, *that* was the film, son. We just filmed it."

"But I did that for just fifty bucks," I said, suddenly flushed with anger. "I gave you a fuck and a movie for just fifty bucks?"

"Read the contract, son. You are bought and paid for in this film. But, no worries," he went on, seeing that I was about to explode, "there will be other films. You'll make good money in those. You are one hot piece of ass."

I took the fifty off the desk, tucked it into my jeans,

and just turned and walked out of the room, not knowing how much of what he was telling me was bullshit. I should have trusted my instincts when I'd entered the room, except, instead of hanging onto my wallet around him, I should have held onto my jeans zipper.

I knew just what he should call his damn film: *Twice Taken*. Once in the ass and once in the wallet.

When I left the room, Leon was waiting for me out in the hall. I have no idea when in the process of my double fuck he'd left the room.

"I'm sure he'll call you back for another film, Brian," Leon said. "I can tell he really liked your stage presence."

"Yeah, well, I think my stage presence is worth more than fifty books," I shot back. I would have said more, but Leon was still my conduit to Rex Reeson when he returned from France.

"Well, if you really need more money, Brian, I think I could set you up in something temporarily."

"Yeah, what would that be?" I tried not to sneer, but I'm not sure how well I succeeded.

"When we were chatting back in the office, you told me you were a dancer in a club briefly on the East Coast. I know of a club that could use someone like you."

Here we go again, I thought. That "use it" part. But Hunter Elliott had also taught me that attaining the goal was more important than saving my dignity if I genuinely wanted to become a Hollywood actor.

"What sort of club?" I asked.

"It's called Thunder Road," Leon answered. "Sort of a men's club with men dancers and waiters."

Yep, here we go again, I thought. But what I said was "It isn't near any naval bases, I hope."

"No, no, it's not," Leon answered. And he gave me the strangest look. I didn't bother to explain, however.

Chapter 4: Shelving Time

Thunder Road was a good couple of steps above Norfolk's Bad Boys' Den in terms of what I had to do for the money. The troupe of male dancers at the Los Angeles club were an offshoot of a permanent revue act at one of the casinos in Las Vegas. And I hadn't been working for more than a couple of weeks at the Los Angeles club before I was asked if I wanted to join the troupe in Las Vegas. But the money right where I was was pretty good. It wasn't bad in the Los Angeles club and there was no backstage fuck room there like there had been in Norfolk—and I didn't have to leave to do a trick with any of the customers I didn't want to. Most important, though, I was still waiting for my big break in movies. And I was still waiting for Rex Reeson to return to the States and help make that happen. I also was waiting for these in Los Angeles. So Las Vegas didn't figure in my immediate future.

Leon, Reeson's West Coast personal assistant, had said I could move in with him until Reeson returned from France to save on my expenses. But Leon seemed just a bit too eager for me to do that. The way he looked at me made me want to step back so I didn't get saliva all down the front of my shirt. And although I couldn't turn him against me, I bore him a grudge for having sent me to give it up in a porn film for only

$50—and, not least, I didn't like the idea that he attended that filming and seemed to enjoy watching me being doubly taken.

But my pride and suspicion didn't extend as far as not to take him up on an offer to bunk and share apartment expenses with a nice-looking guy named Zane who Leon said was already working with Reeson the same way Leon was sure I'd be able to work with Reeson.

Zane was urbane and sophisticated. He drove a Porsche Boxster and dressed like a male model and had the body and looks to go with it. He told me he'd graduated from an Ivy League college back east, and I believed him. But like half of the guys like him—and like me, I guess—in town who were on the make, what he showed up front didn't bear out in where we had to bunk out and the food we could afford to eat.

He was good at tennis and handball, and Reeson had him listed at a good sports club. Leon managed a pass for me too, so, between my male dancing at Thunder Road and the frequent workouts with Zane—and the cost of food in this town—I managed to keep in tip-top shape.

Zane sniffed around me off and on while I was living with him, but he did so in a sort of cursory fashion. One day he'd be eyeing me up and down and giving me "that look" and the next, after he'd put in a all-nighter somewhere, all he seemed to want to do was sleep, and he paid little attention to me at all. I never figured out what he did—what he worked at—until a few weeks after Reeson had returned. But I figured out whatever it was could be pretty exhausting and sometimes made him crabby. The only conversations we had that went beyond the surface revealed that he had just about the same goals as I did—to make it big in movies in Hollywood—but that somehow he'd strayed off the path. He was taking accounting classes at a local community college at night. He said this was to have some hope of getting off the tread mill before he got paunchy and fell off it. I asked him why he hadn't majored in something useful at the Ivy League college of his, and he just laughed at me and said that I probably wouldn't be able to understand what a degree from a college like that was meant to do.

I couldn't help looking at him and seeing that this would be me in a couple of years unless I stuck to pushing my goals. I kept thinking back to what the actor Hunter Elliott back in southern Virginia had counseled me to do—to use all of my wiles, everything available to me, to reach for that gold ring. And I became focused on doing that with Reeson—whenever he returned. The stage director and lover who had given me the recommendation to Reeson had said Reeson would want me. I decided that I had to make that happen.

I just didn't know if I would have to give out to Leon too before I could get to Reeson. Leon made no bones about letting me know he wanted me—badly. And he was a little crass about how he let me know he did. I did what I could not to be alone in a room with him.

About six weeks after I'd arrived in Los Angeles, the long-awaited return of Rex Reeson happened. But I didn't know about it for two more weeks.

One afternoon, out of frustration, I went to Reeson's offices in person to quiz Leon on when his boss was expected.

"Rex?" Leon asked. "Oh, he came back a couple of weeks ago."

"A couple of weeks ago?" I blurted out, barely able to control myself. "You know I've been waiting around just to see him. Did you give him my letter of recommendation from Martin Blixen?"

"I could do that, I suppose," Leon said. And then he gave me a lascivious smile. "Of course, that would be a big favor. I'd need something really worthwhile in return, something that really showed appreciation."

I stood there, bunching up my fists, knowing I was trapped, but not liking it one little bit. I knew exactly what Leon wanted. I was afraid this would be the case. Just how badly did I want this opportunity?

As luck would have it, I had accosted Leon in the hall outside his office before we'd gotten into his private space. And as opportunity would have it, while we were squaring off in the hallway, the double doors at the end of the hall opened and a man appeared who could only be Rex Reeson. From his demeanor and the way he held himself, he obviously was the boss of everything within sight. He was a distinguished-looking man who was probably in his late fifties but who paid big bucks to keep himself ahead of the middle-age spread and race to deterioration. He was a tall man, a good six foot three, and slender, and he had a good tan and a healthy mane of silver hair. He was dressed impeccably in a three-piece suit, he was smiling broadly, and he had a young hunk on each arm.

"Ah, who do we have here?" he said as soon as he spied Leon and me engaging in our tense hallway negotiations. "Just where have you been keeping yourself, angel?"

He had his eyes on me, so I assumed he was talking to me rather than Leon. Leon opened his mouth to speak, but I was already in my "use it" mode. I flashed him a big welcoming smile and jumped into the opportunity with both feet.

"My name is Brian Hinton, Mr. Reeson," I started off in the best stage voice I could muster. "I'm an actor from the East Coast. I recently worked under the Broadway director Martin Blixen, and he suggested that I come see you—that you could help me find my way in movies here. I've been waiting here for you to return from Cannes; I have a letter from Martin here, if—"

"Recommended by Martin, eh, and you served under him, you say?"

We both knew what I had meant by that. I hadn't worded it that way by accident; I was counting on Blixen having been right about what Reeson was interested in. It was definitely "use it" time, or the opportunity very well might slip away. "Yes, sir," I said. And I fluttered my long eyelashes for him and looked as yummy as I could muster. "And I'd be ever so grateful for any help you could give me."

"We're just going out to the house for swim—this is Jules here on my right and Jacques here at my other side. I found them in France and thought they would be useful here. You could join us if you like, and we could discuss . . . possibilities."

When we were in the back of the limo, having left a noticeably seething Leon behind, Reeson came right to his point.

"You said you'd be grateful for help, Brian, my boy. Perhaps you'd like to be grateful to this. I'd like to see what talent this is that Martin thought worthy of a recommendation." As he said that, he was unzipping his fly, and he pulled out a respectably long and thick, half-hard cock. He spread his legs and I dutifully sank down on my knees between his thighs and took his cock in my mouth.

Hunter Elliott had taught me well how to give good suck, and in quick order, Reeson was leaning back into the well-cushioned seat, with his head flung back and his fingers playing in my hair and making purring and gurgling sounds.

I heard him say something to his two French protégés in French and felt eager hands at my waist, undoing my belt and pulling my trousers down and off my legs. While the limo floated up into the Hollywood Hills, Jules and Jacques, in turn, fucked me from behind while I continued to suck Reeson off.

We swam in the nude, and Reeson, standing in a couple of feet of water at the shallow end of the pool, fucked me as I lay on the edge of the pool, my spread legs dangling in the water. And then he watched with interest—and took a couple of hundred rapid photo shots—as Jules fucked me on a lounger and I sucked Jacques off.

"So, I guess Martin Blixen continues to be a good judge of man flesh, Brian, my boy," Reeson said with a little laugh and big smile when we were all mellowed out and taking the sun on loungers at the side of the pool.

"Does that mean you can help me?" I asked.

"Oh, yes, I can help you," Reeson answered. "You're a natural. You'll do very well."

"What studio were you thinking of," I asked—in perhaps my last naïve moment in life.

"Studio?" Reeson asked in a surprised voice. And then he laughed. "I run a male escort service, Brian. A very, very highly paid stable of hunks like you for only the richest and most demanding of men. Have you ever worked for an escort service, Brian?"

I was in shock, but my mind was going lickety-split,

trying its best to make lemonade out of these lemons, assessing the realistic options and trying to hone in on the least undesirable. This had been the only contact I'd been set up with. I could kick myself for my naiveté, and if Blixen had been within striking distance of my fists, I would have throttled him to death. In his own way Hunter had tried to warn me. He'd had a very peculiar reaction when I told him the recommendation Blixen had given me was to Reeson—and I was too naïve and raw to pick up on that.

"Yes," I answered—truthfully, "but that had only been a means to getting out here. I'm an actor, I want—"

"Of course you're an actor, son." Reeson blustered. "And you damn well better be a good actor for what you're going to be doing if you come with me. And I don't care what you do with your spare time. I just want your ass in good working order and your body well taken care of—and a bit of your precious time. And for that, you can be making $2,500 an hour."

Whoa. $2,500 an hour? Already my mind was doing the two step over my druthers and starting to spin out rationalizations and reversing direction. Just like in Norfolk, this didn't have to be forever. But $2,500 an hour. Whoa!

It didn't take me long to ask when and how I started.

"It will be a couple of months before you can be fully groomed and prepared," Reeson said. "But you've got a good start. You've got something special, something natural. Some more schooling and some guidance and instruction, and you can be pulling in those big bucks and going to school at night if you want or even fitting in some time for acting roles, if that's what you've really got your heart set on and you can manage to land the parts. We've got some big-time directors and producers on our client list, so there's always a chance you can get in through the back door like that. It's certainly happened before."

This was sounding less and less of a diversion from my goals than I had been thinking.

Reeson was continuing to talk, though. "We'll get you with Zane. He can shape you up in no time, I'm sure. And will be sensitive about it. We don't want to train that natural vulnerability and charisma out of you."

"Zane!" I didn't even know I had blurted it out aloud, until Reeson parroted it back at me.

"Yes, Zane. He's one of our best. I can arrange—"

"I'm already bunking with someone named Zane," I said, interrupting him, something I'd never do if I wasn't running along the edge of shock. "Leon arranged for me to share an apartment with a guy named Zane, a blond dude who drives a Porsche. You don't suppose . . . ? I wonder how many Zane's there can be in this town."

"Yep, that sounds like our Zane to me," Reeson said. Then he laughed again. "That Leon; he always stays two steps ahead of me. He's been setting this up all along, I'll wager. Just as well. It will be Leon who gives you your assignments."

I was coming down off that high already. I should have known that Leon came with the deal. But, still, $2,500 a fucking hour for something I'd been giving away for $50 a throw. . . .

Chapter 5: Men in Tuxedos

"Man, don't you ever give up?" I asked in exasperation, removing Zane's hand from my basket, rising from the sofa, and moving over to a stool by the bar. I was going to put out for Zane, but I didn't think he'd been told yet that he was going to be mentoring me for Rex Reeson's stable of male escorts, and I wanted him to work for it a bit more. Besides, there were a couple of things I wanted to ask him about while I had some hope of getting an honest answer.

"No, Brian, I never give up. Not when there's something I want like I want you."

"I should have known when you brought out the good scotch that you just wanted to get me drunk and have your way with me. True?" I'd already let Zane kiss me when I'd come back from my signup session with Reeson and his French sidekicks, so we both knew I was just playing with him now.

"Yes, that was the general idea," Zane said dryly, a smile of perseverance on his lips. "What's the problem? You don't find me attractive?"

"Yeah, you're plenty attractive all right, Zane," I said. Still, I tried to put a glint of defiance in my eyes—trying to work in some acting on him. "And well you know it to. I just don't open my legs for anyone who says he wants me."

"You sure open them for the customers down at Thunder Road," Zane retorted, the smile just as sparkly as before.

"That's different," I said. "And I don't do much of that there anyway."

"Right. They have money and position and are proper sugar daddies. You're so obviously on the make for connections to give you a start in movies. You know what that kind of arrangement is called, don't you?"

"Yeah, that's called good old American trade," I shot back. "Quality goods for quality services. And I see no reason for you or anyone else to look down your nose at it."

"Oh, I'm not," Zane answered calmly. "Believe me I'm there myself."

"Excuse me?" I said. I gave him the surprised and intrigued act. I had learned he was in the trade, but he'd never said as much to me himself until now. He had acted as if that was below him. "You of the Ivy League education and Porsche Boxster and expensive clothes?"

"Right," Zane responded, getting a glint of an opening here

"So, what do you know of what a guy's got to do to make it in this town?" I challenged. I was going to make him tell me he was a male prostitute working for Reeson and opening his legs on demand, just like he said I was doing at Thunder Road.

"I didn't come from money, Brian," Zane shot back. "I know it looks like I did from my car and clothes and from my education, but I earned my education on my back—just like you are doing at Thunder Road."

"What do you mean?" I wanted him to say it. To tell me something that would open him up to me emotionally before I opened my legs to him and let him fuck me.

"I put myself through school by working for a hard-core call boy service—one that put me out on the street advertising for tricks," Zane said. "I came to this lifestyle through hard work."

There, it had been said. Now to push him just a bit

44

farther. I returned to the sofa and started pelting Zane with some of the questions I wanted answered before I signed up for Reeson's stable. I took a couple of swigs of scotch from the generous portion Zane had poured out for me and settled back in the sofa cushions. I purposely didn't pull away when Zane put a hand on my thigh and started working it up my leg.

"And what was your strangest assignment?" I asked Zane at the end of a flurry of other questions that Zane had dutifully responded to. "I mean, can you remember any? There must have been some." One of the real burning questions I had with this was just how kinky this arrangement might get—and whether it might be more than I thought I could handle.

Zane chewed on that one briefly—but only briefly. He had his hand on my bare belly now, under the hem of my shirt. His other arm was snaked around my shoulder. I acted like I didn't even know his hands were there, letting him play his little seduction game. I knew this would end with him fucking me just as much as he hoped that was where this was going.

"Hmmm, let's see. That might have been the night of the men in the tuxedos."

"The men in the tuxedos?" I said, showing him I was interested and also that talking to me like this would get him what he wanted. To drive that home, I put my hand on top of his and moved it below my waistband, on the warm skin of my lower belly, letting his fingers glide into my pubes. Then he started into his story.

* * * *

"Yes. As the night was starting out, I knew I was in for a workout, because the caller had specified he wanted someone experienced with men and had authorized for the full unlimited service for a four-hour period. That usually meant multiple ass work, although it's true that some out-of-town hicks just didn't realize what the various options were and had more money than brains when they set up a session. I knew there was big money involved, though, because the gig was in New York. I was flown across the country for it.

"The address I was given was for a large, but nondescript brownstone, up on 57th Street, near Central Park. A polished brass plate by the doorbell simply stated that I was at some club, Hedgewood or Hedgeneck, or something like that. I later assumed that it was one of those old-world highly exclusive men's clubs that had existed for a couple of centuries without catching the public eye.

"I was met at the door by the epitome of a butler type who told me to follow him toward the back of the house. Outside a double oaken door set in a whole hallway of polished oaken paneling carpeted with an Oriental rug in vibrant colors, he told me to strip entirely and to leave my clothes folded on a Chippendale arm chair that was located next to the door. I did so, and then he knocked twice on the door, opened it, and ushered me into the room.

"I was in some sort of club room. Leather-upholstered arm chairs sitting on a huge Oriental carpet in the middle of a wood-paneled room with glass-fronted shelves of books on three walls and on the third wall a fireplace flanked by French doors that apparently led to garden at the rear of the building. At the opposite end of the room from the fireplace was a large mahogany desk with a leather top. The arm chairs were arranged in a circle in the center of the room, facing each other, with a clear space out in the center. There were six chairs, each with a little cigarette table beside it and a brass floor lamp behind it. All of the lamp shades were turned up so that they functioned as spotlights trained on the circle in front the chairs. Each of the chairs was occupied by a man in a tuxedo. All of the men were fairly young—none older than his mid forties—and all had the air of pampering to a high gloss and well-toned physiques and of highly successful positions. They had brandy snifters in their manicured and bejeweled hands, and each was smoking a cigar. The air was cloudy with the smell of premium Cuban cigar smoke.

"'Come to the center of the room, please, son,' a strong, willful voice commanded me from the depths of the cigar smoke cloud. I did as I was bade.

"'Turn, please. Turn completely around. Slowly please.

Again please. Stand straight and tall, please. You have nothing to be ashamed of.' I slowly turned a few times, obviously letting them all see what they were paying for, for whatever purpose—which I had yet to discern.

"'Now masturbate for us, please. To completion. Do not worry about where it goes.' The same commanding voice. From the intensity of the light directed from the lamps and the thickness of the cigar smoke, I could not be sure which tuxedo had spoken.

"'Excuse me?' I asked. In shock more at the incongruity of the setting than at the request itself. I had known it would be a performance evening for me. They had paid dearly for it. This assignment would carry me nearly a month at school all by itself.

"'Masturbate, please. And do it slowly and don't hold back on your expression and response, please.'

"So, I did as he commanded. I had been trained what to do with this sort of request, but I had always assumed it would be something involved in a one-on-one situation.

"I was progressing pretty well, when I sensed movement in the room behind me, and I heard the rustle of rich material close behind me and hot breath on my neck. I looked down, and an arm came around me from behind. It was clothed in luxurious black material. White starched cuffs showed at the wrist, with gold nugget cuff links. An elegant, manicured hand with a signet ring wrapped itself around my engorged cock after brushing my hand away.

"Another black-clad figure was now at the other side of me. I turned enough to see the brilliant white shirt front and the satiny lapel on the tuxedo. The hand of this figure also went to my cock, and the two tuxedos worked my cock in unison and rubbed their expensive evening suits against my bare arms.

"Another figure, a commanding figure, probably the source of the voice that had given me direction, appeared through the cloud of smoke before me. He was sucking on a long cigar and giving me a very intense look. He was perhaps the oldest of the men present. Very handsome, with strong facile features and intense black eyes. The light was reflecting off the diamond studs cascading down the front of his perfectly cut tuxedo. I remember thinking that one of those studs alone would be enough to get me out of the business and would cover the rest of my college. He gave me a grin, almost a leer, and then he turned the cigar in his mouth, took it out, and pressed it between my lips. It was moist from his saliva. He rotated it in my mouth, adding my saliva to his, and then he grinned again and moved out of my line of vision.

"He obviously had moved to behind me, because I felt hands pulling my butt cheeks apart—in fact I found hands everywhere on my thighs and belly and nipples, in addition to the two that were stroking my cock—and I bowed my legs outward as I felt the moist end of the cigar working its way into my ass.

"The heel of a hand came up under my chin, the fingers covering my lower jaw and the thumb pushing its way into my mouth, obviously wanting me to give suck, which I did. Meanwhile, the two hands were still stroking my cock, the fingers of both of my hands were being taken into mouths and sucked, and that cigar was being rotated in my ass, being screwed in deeper and deeper and rotated around.

"I was panting heavily at the attention, the feeling of being shrouded in elegant black satin and silks and white starched shirts, flashing studs, and heavy cigar smoke. Aroused by the contrast of my being completely naked and vulnerable and being stroked and invaded everywhere by fully and elegantly clothed men.

"The cigar twisted out of my ass, and the commanding figure came back around to close in front of me. He gave me that leering, possessive smile, and then he put the cigar back in his mouth and twisted it. His eyes lit up with a mischievous gleam and I felt a strong hand cupping my balls, coming in under the stroking hands of other tuxedos, and he squeezed hard. I threw my head up in a primeval scream of pain and surprise and release to the ceiling, jerking my mouth away from the thumb I was sucking, and shot a strong fountain of semen I know not where.

"The teeming mass of black silk and satin took my ejaculation as some sort of sign, because I was lifted and carried by a bevy of tuxedos over to the leather-topped mahogany desk. At first I was bent over that on my belly. Once again hands pulled my cheeks wide. Then fingers, slippery with lubrication, of different sizes, invaded me, pulling my well-used hole wide. The cigar again now, soggy with lubricant, entering between the fingers and twirling and screwing into me. I was panting and moaning. The cigar twirled out, but the three fingers of different sizes remained, pulling me, stretching my hole wide. I arched my back, as a thicker, throbbing object, a cock, slid in between the fingers. The fingers pulled out as the cock plowed in, deeper, deeper, deeper. And then it started a furious rhythmic slapping back and forth into me as I counterthrusted my hips back to it until I heard a deep-throated cry and felt my insides being creamed. A second cock replaced the first and I was fucked vigorously and deeply from the rear by one cock while another tuxedoed figure on the other side of the desk pushed another cock into my mouth. At no time did I see man flesh during the whole ritual. Cocks were buried in my ass and mouth, but the tuxedos remained fully in place otherwise.

"I was fully naked, being fully possessed by six elegant tuxedos, heavy, hard, virile cocks invading me from within the folds of the rich material, but never seen.

"When the first set of tuxedos had spent its seed in either end of me, I was turned on my back and fucked repeatedly in succession, each man obviously taking more than one turn at me, with two tuxedos holding my arms out and two more spread-eagling my legs.

"As something of a finale, I was lifted off the desk and a tuxedo came in under me and settled me on his black silk lap, his cock buried in my ass, and another tuxedo came in at me from the front and penetrated me with his member as well. The most athletic of the tuxedos was hunched on top of the desk, black silk pant legs against my naked chest and me deep-throating his cock, chaffing my chin and cheeks on the zipper of the only slightly parted fly.

49

"I found myself draped, naked, and covered with repeated semen of six men over the top of the desk, moaning my elegant defilement, trying to concentrate on the fee I had earned for the evening. When I was able, I pulled myself up to a sitting position. The six chairs once more were occupied by six sedately and richly clad gentlemen sipping their brandy and puffing their cigars and looking very satiated and pleased with themselves.

"The commanding voice then thanked me for my time and told me I was to leave. I dragged myself out into the hall, dressed with my aching muscles feeling every move, and received a generous tip from the butler before I was shown to the door."

* * * *

When Zane had finished this story, the room was silent for the longest moment except for the heavy panting coming from me, and not just from the sensuous tale he had spun, but because, while telling the story, he had pulled me over close to him and leaned both of us down on the sofa and his hand was completely below my waist band and was encircling my cock. I found myself fully aroused by his story, not put off at all by the kinkiness of it—drawn to it, somewhat frustrated that it had been his experience, not mine.

"Yes, I think that might have been my strangest assignment," Zane said finally, marking closure to his tale.

"Wow." That seemed to be all I could say at the moment. I was breathing too heavily to contribute much to sophisticated conversation.

Zane sensed he had me now, and I was completely ready for him. I unzipped my fly myself, and Zane correctly took that as a sign that he could bring my cock out into the open, which he did, and began to stroke it.

"So, what do you think?" He asked

A few more moments of silence except for my soft moaning and sighing and the rustle of the cheap cotton material of my pants in its rhythmic countermovement to

Zane's slow stroking motion.

"You wouldn't . . . You wouldn't happen to own a tuxedo?" I asked in a hoarse, struggled whisper.

"Why, yes. Yes I do. I think I can find a box of fine Cuban cigars too," Zane said just before I lifted my lips to his and sank into a deep, passionate, moaning kiss.

Zane didn't know it yet, but his indoctrination of me for Reeson's escort service had already been quite successfully launched. Within a few short weeks under his guidance, I was to become a full-fledged member of the Reeson team and would start collecting melting stories of assignments all my own.

Chapter 6: B-6 Cowboy Special

My eyes just about rolled up into my head when I came on duty and Leon handed me a ticket for a B-6 Cowboy Special.

"I might have to take something to reload that fast unless they're all content with a mouth or finger job, Leon," I said as I stripped and started to pour myself into the cowboy costume.

"Naw, that's why I saved that ticket for you," Leon said with a short little laugh. "You've got the reputation for keepin' it hard the longest of any we've got on the rolls. It'll mean a good $400 evening for you, with six specials added to the base $100 just for lettin' 'em look a ya. Just think of all the dough you'll be making."

Leon was just about drooling as he watched me fold my well-hung piece into the pouch under the breakaway pants, slip into the breakaway shirt, and start strapping on the chaps. I'd learned a long time ago what Leon liked and wanted from the guys on the rolls—even though he still wasn't getting it from me, much to his chagrin.

Well, after I'd done six bachelorettes at this party assignment, there wouldn't be much left to share with Leon when I returned, even if I wanted to. But he was right. $400 for a B-6 Special—a bachelorette striptease party with six sex acts I'd have to perform—was really good money for one evening's work if I could hack it. It would just about cover that work I had to have done to my Mustang.

I looked at the address on my ticket. The party was in the wedding suite of a local upscale hotel. It was Friday now, so I assumed they'd booked the suite for the duration of the wedding festivities, and this was the bride's last fling. Must be shelling out a lot of dough for this affair, I thought. That wedding suite didn't come cheaply. And neither did I.

"I guess the girls in the wedding party want to sow their last oats before one of them takes the big plunge," I said, as I put my arms through the cowhide vest and tied a red bandana around my neck.

"These are the guys in the wedding party, not the girls. This is a bachelor party," Leon said with great satisfaction, giving me a leer.

"Ouch," I exclaimed. I bet Leon had given me this assignment with a great deal of pleasure. I was one of the only guys who pretty much spurned his suggestions for coupling up. Well, at least this would probably mean I wouldn't have to be worrying about reloading five times in a short period. The only surprise was that this escort service had added the B category to answer the demand from the women. This was the first one I'd heard of that was booked by men. The service usually did cater to the men otherwise.

I could tell the party was already going strong when I arrived at the wedding suite door. I took off the overcoat that had covered my cowboy costume while I'd scurried through the lobby and up the elevator and knocked on the door. The young blond stud who answered the door and gave me a big welcoming smile was minimally dressed in just gym shorts and a beer can in his hand, but, as he pulled me inside, I could see that he was overdressed compared to the other four studs scattered about the suite. They only sported the beer cans— and impressive hard-ons.

Blondie cranked up the music and had me going right into my regular striptease routine. They cheered and saluted as the breakaway pants came off and then the shirt, leaving me only in the boots, chaps, vest, bandana, and the skimpy pouch.

The guy who was obviously the groom-to-be, a dark-haired muscle stud, swarthy of complexion and intriguing decorated with curly hair on various parts of his body and who might have been the quarterback of this team, wanted a lap dance as soon as I had stripped down to the minimal costume. When I came down into his lap as he was sitting in a straight chair, he minimalized the costume further by jerking off my pouch. He palmed our cocks together and stroked them as I rubbed my nipples against his, reveling in the soft silkiness of his chest hair, and went into a deep lip lock. All the time I was thinking that the basic $100—which was half the $200 they had to pay for the basic striptease—was earned and now I was moving into earning my $50 share of the $100 for the first sex act. This wasn't going to be so bad. The groom-to-be was quite desirable.

In fact, this guy was really turning me on, and my cock hardened right up to his attention. I knew I was going to get a hot ride and I even was going to be paid for it. We were both panting and moaning to beat the band, and he had his lips on my nipples, when two of his attendants got on either side of me and lifted me by the thighs and, after crowning him with a condom, set me down on the groom's cock. I cried out in ecstasy as my ass canal sheathed his thick, throbbing tool, and the groomsmen just kept lifting and lowering my pelvis on the groom's dick until he gave a little scream and ballooned out the condom inside me with his cum.

They gave me no rest, though; the two groomsmen carried me, still gripping me by my thighs, into the adjoining bedroom and laid me on my back at the foot of a four-poster bed. The two of them strapped my legs to the posts with leather belts so that my legs were spread out wide, and then they took turns, in the paid-for sex acts two and three, adding their probing dicks to the exploration of my ass the groom had just accomplished. The end of the bed was facing a large dresser mirror, and the groom had come up on the bed behind me and pillowed my head in his lap, which elevated it enough that I could watch the undulation of the firm, melon-round butts of the two stud groomsmen in the mirror as they pumped my asshole. Once again I congratulated myself on both having a wild fuck and being richly rewarded for doing so.

The groom, obviously smitten with me, was making little mewing sounds to me while his hands and lips explored my upper body. I lay there, writhing under the attention of the groom and his attendants, as the two groomsmen who had carried me into the room and strapped me to the bedposts fucked me deep, one after the other. A third groomsman, a big black stud who had held back from the group as I was being pumped up and down on the groom's cock in the other room, approached between my legs when his two cohorts were done and sucked my cock until I spouted off with a little scream of ecstasy. Then he, too, added his attention to the collection in my ass canal and pistoned his cock inside me endlessly until, with a sigh of satisfaction, he came and melted away from sight.

Then acts five and six came simultaneously, as the blond hunk, who had been revealed to me as being the best man, unstrapped my legs and turned me on my stomach. My mouth was brought to the groom's reengorged cock, and I sucked him off in deep-throated strokes, as the best man proved to be true to his name in both the length and girth of his cock and pumped me doggie style for the next half hour.

I left the wedding suite hours after I had arrived, walking bowlegged from the attention my ass had received from the five muscle studs but with $400 in cash in my coat pocket for me and $400 for Leon and with smiles all around.

It was with a sense of surprise but not regret the next evening when Leon handed me a ticket for a B-2 Cowboy Special at the same hotel wedding suite at midnight the next night. All I could think of as I drove across town was that these guys were really randy and wondering what two guys I'd drawn. My guess was it was the groom and best man, the studliest of the lot, on the reasoning that they would be the ones most likely to hanging out in the wedding suite.

When the door was opened to my knock, I went into a

56

broad smile that matched that of the guy who answered the door—the hunky groom. I had drawn a long straw with that. But I was thoroughly surprised when I entered the room and found that the other occupant was not the best man; it obviously was the bride.

"What . . . ?" I stammered.

"This is Glynnis," the groom explained. "Last night was one of several tryouts. You won in a breeze. This is our wedding night, and I promised Glynnis it would really be special."

Still in shock, I performed my standard cowboy striptease and then the groom took both his new bride and me by the hand and drew us into the bedroom.

At his invitation, I fucked his bride in the wedding four-poster bed missionary style, while he fucked me from behind. From the sounds of our three-point harmony in cries and groans and moans, it was a wedding night for us all to remember. I left hours—and several hot couple combinations—later, having given them my wedding present of several rounds of off-the-clock fuckings, thinking that this was going to be the most open marriage I'd ever heard about— and hoping that they would be becoming regular customers.

Chapter 7: Taking the High Road

Raindrops were beginning to splatter against the windshield and distant thunder promised more bombast as I reached a Y in the road I hadn't expected and was forced, in view of the lights bearing down on me from a vehicle somewhere in back and near to me, to make a decision. "Take the high road" wafted through my brain. I had no idea why I had remembered that now, but it had been a favorite expression of my Scottish grandfather, and it offered me more direction at the moment than anything else I had on offer. So, I turned right, uphill. I only saw a glimpse of the signpost in the gloom, set off at a useless angle, as I passed it, but I caught "Timber" something or other. I put the slip of paper I had up to the dashboard lights to refresh my memory. It said "Timberlake 760," so I thanked my grandfather for direction and gunned the motor to ascend the steep side of the hill.

I was a little irritated and on edge about this call out tonight. The call had come late, I had other plans, and it was going to storm a bitch tonight. Leon had given me the assignment slip, and I'd seen that it was an M-4 Regular Cowboy. All three elements combined to bode problems. The "M" was OK in its own right, but four of them meant there were few enough to indicate they might be rough and more than

I could handle if they did get frisky. Under the circumstances, the "Regular" gave me pause too, especially in conjunction with the "Cowboy." When "Cowboy" was specified, the fantasy it provided usually ended with someone wanting to fuck someone—and if they hadn't paid for a "Special" up front, it often meant they knew they wanted it to end that way but didn't want to pay up front—or at all—for the special service. Often enough it would be some guy who thought so much of himself that he was sure I would want to give it all up to him for free just because I couldn't resist him.

Thankfully tonight was supposed to be a double. Freddie had come up the mountain a bit ahead of me. At least there would be two of us. But I wasn't sure about that either. Freddie had bailed out on me before and left me to handle everything myself. Twice. I had half a notion to bail out on him tonight. I had a bad feeling about this assignment.

It was getting darker and the thunder was coming closer. There were few houses on this mountainside overlooking L.A. and the ocean. It was an exclusive section and the people living here could afford their privacy. No lights on the road and few address boards large enough to be read from the street, particularly not at night. But I could tell I was in the 700 block now, and, with difficulty, coasting slowly as the rain drops hitting the windshield got larger and larger, I picked out the number 760 and pulled into a pebbled driveway that turned me almost completely around as it dipped down to a small boxy log-sided building pushed into the side of a sharp drop off. A two-car garage was sunk into the hillside at the left of the parking apron that went to the right up to a sheer drop off. Nothing about the place looked inviting, and I didn't see Freddie's Corvette. So, he had abandoned me again, it seemed.

I was furious. Not just at Freddie, but because they hadn't even left a light on beside the door in the blank, windowless wall. There were no windows on the drive side on either story, and the place looked small and abandoned. I was going to dance for four guys in a place like this, and they hadn't paid for sex on top of the dance. And Freddie wouldn't even be there to back me up. Terrific. But an assignment was an assignment, and if I bugged out I would be out my money—and Leon's goodwill. And if Leon was mad at me, I'd probably get an even worse assignment the next time.

I climbed out of the BMW, adjusted my breakaway shirt and pants and the chaps, put the ten-gallon hat on, set my professional face in place, and slammed the car door shut. As if on signal, the heavens picked that moment for the first deluge marking the oncoming storm, and I was drenched before I hit the door.

It was several minutes before the light came on beside the door. I was soaked to the skin and this would be the most revealing entrance I will have ever made to such an assignment. Breakaway clothes didn't leave much to the imagination when they were soaked. I was this far from returning to the car and roaring out of there when the door opened.

I recognized him in an instant. It was Ted Thorenson, that director of several very popular television situation dramas. And it was a very surprised Ted Thorenson. He obviously wasn't expecting anyone. He was barefoot and encased in a plush velour robe. His hair was tussled as if he had just gotten out of bed. That impression was only strengthened when I looked past him into what was essentially a one-room cottage with an enormous double-sided stone fireplace between the two living spaces. I could see past the fireplace to an large bed that was as tussled as Thorenson looked and was lumpy with strewn pillows and disordered sheets and spread.

And there weren't three other guys at the door salivating for an exotic Cowboy dance.

Thorenson's expression turned from surprise to amusement and then to something else—to something I was entirely too familiar with in my dealing with clients.

He was interested. I had come to Hollywood with a dream of auditioning with such as Thorenson and I'd never even gotten into the outer office of a director at his level. A quickie porn movie leading to employment with an escort service was the best I'd gotten. And here I was, soaked, standing on the threshold of Ted Thorenson's hillside hideaway cottage, and looking silly in a transparent Cowboy getup. Charming. I had known this wasn't going to be a good night.

"760 Timberlake?" I asked in a hoarse voice. It was all I could think of asking.

"No, sorry," Thorenson responded in a British-accent voice that probably melted all of his conquests, of which I'd heard there were many. Thorenson was a handsome man. He was well into his fifties, but he had kept extraordinarily good care of himself and was quite distinguished looking, which had only been enhanced when his temples had gone gray. And he still had all of the power and presence of robust strength about him that extended from his early days as a Hollywood stunt man and movie hunk.

"This is 760 Timberwood," he continued. "It's a common mistake; you should have turned downhill on Timberlake back at the split in the road."

"Oh, sorry. Wrong house." I started to turn to leave, but he put his hand on my arm, and as he did so, his robe parted, and I saw that he had a heavily muscled barrel of a chest with a profusion of black and gray chest hair.

"You're soaked," he said gently, but with an air of authority. "Come inside and get dry and warm up before you proceed. You'll get your death of cold otherwise."

I let him draw me into the house, which looked like heaven from where I was standing out in the rain on the blank-walled pebbled entry. Once inside, I saw that the house wasn't a claustrophobic walled-in box at all. The two walls away from the drive and the hillside were entirely of glass. Two stories of glass overlooking the blinking lights of the city and the dark ocean beyond. And the furnishings were lush cordovan leather and pine furniture, with the colors of yellow, red, orange, and brown predominating, bringing a warm glow to the interior that was enhanced by the roaring fire in the dominating stone fireplace. To the right of where I now stood just inside the door was a living area, with a brown leather sectional sofa and heavy wool rugs in earth tones on a highly polished random-width pine floor. To the left was a dining area with pine furniture and a wall of kitchen cabinets with pine doors and red-tile countertops. The bedroom area was beyond the fireplace, in the corner of the two high window walls overlooking the city. The bathroom and dressing area was walled off from there on the side of the building pushed into the hillside. Above that was a loft area, which looked like it was set up as Thorenson's hideaway office.

"Come, get out of those drenched clothes before you flood my floor," Thorenson said with a smile. "Water would be murder on this wooden floor. I just had it installed."

"Sorry. But my other clothes are back in the car," I said nonsensically.

"And if you go back for them, they'll only get drenched too," Thorenson said. And then he laughed. "Here, those are hardly clothes anyway. Quite a getup."

"Uh, sorry," I said, and I started to unlace the chaps. I didn't know what else to say. What can one say who unexpectedly shows up at a Hollywood director's door on a rainy night in a breakaway cowboy outfit?

"Quite nice, actually," Thorenson said. "From the Thunder Road club, aren't you?"

Shock. He knew. But somehow that made me relax. If he knew, then this wasn't going to be as awkward as I feared.

"Yes, sorry," I said. It seemed all I could do was apologize. I had the chaps and boots off. The shirt and pants, of course, were the easy party. They were designed to come up with just a tug.

"Here's a towel. And, here, then put this robe on." He was stripping off the velour robe and all he had on underneath were a pair of short sleeping pants. I had, indeed, brought him from his bed. And I could see now that my impressions were right. He was still in magnificent shape for his age.

"Oh, I couldn't. You shouldn't . . ."

But he already had and I could. I had dried off, and he had the robe draped around my shoulders. The scent of him— a musky, wood smoke sensation—was arousing.

"Come on over and sit at the table. I'll fix some coffee to warm you, and then you can shower."

"I can't, really," I stammered. "I have a gig I've got to

get to."

"Down on Timberlake?" He asked as he led me to a chair at the table, sat me down, and moved off into the kitchen. He moved like a cat. Feline and fluid, even though he was solidly built, with heavy, but well-proportioned muscles.

He quickly had the coffee going and then went off into the bedroom area, leaving me alone waiting to politely thank him but saying that I had to get back on the road. The rain had stopped, although the rumbling of the thunder, louder now than before, promised more—and heavier—to come. The guys down on Timberlake wouldn't care if the cowboy outfit was wet. I'd just thank Thorenson for his hospitality and leave.

He was nattering on about how easy it was to confuse Timberlake and Timberwood drives, especially at night, and how they should change one of the names, as he pattered back from the bedroom area. He laid some red plaid material on the table and went back into the kitchen area, where the coffee was now finished perking. He wasn't giving me an in to give my thank-you and good-bye speech. And then he was back at the table and set a cup of coffee in front of me and a wallet in front of his chair and sat down.

"Thanks. You've been great," I started. "But I really must . . ."

"How much were you going to be paid on Timberlake for a dance?" he asked abruptly.

"Two hundred" I said, so surprised that I just answered him straight out.

"And was that for a fuck, too?" he asked.

"No," I said, completely flustered now. "Just for the dance. Nothing else was booked."

"And if they did fuck you, how much would that be?"

"A hundred each," I responded. "There are supposed to be four there. They might not all want it; they didn't book that, but . . ."

Thorenson opened the wallet and took out seven hundred-dollar notes. "There," he said, as he laid them in front of me on the table. "Now, is there any real reason to go to Timberlake Drive tonight?"

"No . . . no, I guess not," I stammered.

"OK, then. Drink your coffee and go have that shower and come back into the bedroom wearing these." He lifted up the material he'd placed on the table to reveal that it was a Scottish kilt. And under that were a pair of white knee-high socks with red garters.

"A Scottish costume?" I asked, dumfounded.

"You came in a costume. Any objection to wearing one I've provided when I fuck you?" Thorenson asked. He was nothing if not straightforward.

"No, I guess not. No, of course not." Then I smiled for him, turning on my studied charm. He was just another trick now—and, just maybe, an audition possibility for that movie role I was still dreaming about. I didn't really care what fetishes he did or didn't have. He certainly was easier to handle than four guys down on Timberlake.

I showered and dried myself off and then put on the kilt he gave me, which was slung low in front. Then I put on the white knit socks, with the tops folded over the red garters just below my knees. I look at myself in the full-length mirror beside the shower and decided that I didn't look half bad. I'd have to suggest this getup to Leon to add to the escort service's exotic costume collection. Thorenson hadn't given me anything to wear under the kilt, so he obviously wanted me ready for action.

When I came out of the bathroom, I found, with a shock, that it hadn't been a lump of pillows in Thorenson's bed. It had been Jason Craig. I recognized him right away too. Craig played the teenage son in one of Thorenson's long-running television dramas and had done so for eight seasons. So, he no longer was a teenager in fact, but he somehow had kept his teenage looks. A blond twink's body, with an almost feminine, too pretty for his own good, pouting face with sensuous lips and bedroom eyes. He was the idol of many a pubescent female television viewer.

Now, however, he was on his hairless twink's breast on the bed with his pert little tail up in the air. He was wearing white briefs and nothing else, and Thorenson was sitting on the bed beside him, a bottle of KY in one hand and the index finger of the other hand worrying a small hole on the butt cheek of Craig's briefs. The finger would go in and move around on Craig's flesh and then come out and Thorenson would tear the hole a bit larger and then the finger, and a second one, would go in and the white cotton material would raise in waves where the fingers were exploring. Craig had his face turned to me, and he was giving me a dreamy look.

"Pull that chair over to there," Thorenson directed me in his director's voice, pointing to a spot beside the bed and in front of a bureau, "and sit in the chair and put your legs over the arms. Yes, like that. You look very sexy, by the way. And just watch for a while. You can stroke yourself, but beneath the kilt, please. I like to see the material move and your chest muscles ripple. I like to see movement between material and skin."

Always the detail man, Thorenson, I thought, as I followed his direction. I didn't fondle myself at first, but as I watched Thorenson work on his young protégé in the glow of the roaring fire with the backdrop of the lights of L.A. below and the lights of intermittent lightning from above, I found myself lazily pulling at my tool.

Thorenson had taken off the sleeping shorts, and he was at full, upward-curved, magnificent arousal. He had a cock to be proud of, both longer and thicker than I could manage with mine, and I was no slouch in that department.

I sat and watched in fascination, as Thorenson worked the hole in Craig's briefs open with the two fingers, and then three, while his other hand went up under the leg hole of the briefs and was, presumably, playing with the young actor's cock and balls. Craig was moaning softly and sighing and giving me those "Look how good I'm getting it" eyes. All the time both Thorenson and I were watching the puffing of the material marking where the fingers were gliding. Getting the point of Thorenson's interest in that direction, I gripped my hard cock from underneath and snaked it around under the kilt material, making the material rise and fall and ripple. Thorenson was looking over at me from time to time and licking his lips.

At length Thorenson pulled his fingers out of the enlarged hole in the briefs and slathered them with KY and then inserted them again, and I saw them through the thin material of the briefs move to between Craig's butt cheeks and Craig's eyes and mouth opened wide. He let out a groan as Thorenson entered him with the fingers.

Thorenson looked over at me and smiled. "Enjoying this, I hope," he said. "Ah, yes, I can see you are. Nice work under the kilt there. That's what I like to see. And it looks so good on you. Wonderful definition. You'd look great on the big screen. But here, before you get too comfortable, go over to the nightstand there and get a condom and crown me. You'd best get one for yourself too. You'll need it. And . . . and a second one for me."

I rose and did as he said, tearing open a packet and rolling a condom on his gigantic tool. He brought my head down to his with a hand around my neck and gave me a deep kiss. And then I was back in my chair, legs draped over the arms, and one hand busy under the kilt and the other one working my nipples. Thorenson was sliding a finger in and out of Craig's ass through the hole in the briefs, and Craig was moaning and moving his chest around on the sheets and his ass back and forth on Thorenson's finger.

Craig was panting and so was I. The scene was bathed in light from flashes of lightning outside at not-more-than-one-minute intervals now, and the wind was howling around the cabin perched on the mountainside. Thorenson extracted his finger and, with both hands, rent the hole in the briefs larger. He slathered his sheathed tool with KY, and then he was on his knees behind the raised hips of the young actor and was working his cock inside the hole in the briefs.

I watched, slack jowled, as Thorenson positioned the head of his tool at Craig's rim and then, hands now holding the young man's thighs, slowly entered him. Craig howled with the howling wind outside at the stretching invasion. I don't know how much of it was real and how much was acting—much of it was acting, I surmised, as it seemed meant to arouse Thorenson to the limit—but Craig was crying out in agony and passion as

Thorenson plowed up into him. He writhed, and screamed his distress, and begged for mercy and for patience. And then, slowly, these cries turned to cries of passion and for Thorenson to fuck him hard and deep. The young actor was bunching up sheeting in his fists and his mouth and giving me, at first, a wild "help me" look—and then, quickly enough, a self-satisfied, saucy "look what I have and you don't" look.

This hadn't gone on long, though, before Thorenson looked up at me, and in a throaty voice said, "Come and take over for me. Have some fun of your own. Roll that condom on and come on over here."

Fully aroused now, I didn't wait for a second invitation. I nervously tore open the condom packet, sheathed myself, and then hopped over to the bed. As I came over, Thorenson pulled out of Craig's ass and pulled the youth back to where his knees were on the edge of the foot of the bed. I hadn't really liked the look Craig had given me, and I wasn't in a charitable mood, so as soon as I had saddled up to his ass, I thrust inside him with one, long bottoming-out slide. He rewarded me with a cry that wasn't acting. Thorenson had stretched him wider than I could, though, and he was well lubricated, so it was an easy plowing for both of us.

I got my hands on the briefs and just ripped them away so that the young actor's taut little butt cheeks were fully exposed. I rode him hard and slapped at his cheeks, while he gave me noises of being well taken. Meanwhile, Thorenson was on his knees behind me, his head under my kilt and his mouth on my asshole. He was giving me as good and deep a tonguing there as anyone before him had, and his tongue was longer and thicker than some client's cocks. It certainly was bigger than Craig's cock. I had snaked my hand around to the young actor's groin, and I found a boy's cock and balls. He had a young twink's cock, although it was enlarging more as I worked it, and it wasn't long before he had ejaculated into the palm of my hand.

I leaned my head down to his then, and he turned his face and gave me a deep kiss with those famous sensuous lips, showing me that he had enjoyed my visit.

While we were kissing, Thorenson stood up and was running his cock up and down my now-enlarged hole, dry fucking me between my butt cheeks. On one of the passes, though, he turned the bulbous head of his cock so that it was pushing at the rim of my hole, and then I was crying out just as Craig had done, without an ounce of acting, of being fully taken, as he entered me. He turned his cock around and from side to side to open me farther as he relentlessly bored up into me. And I cried out and groaned and moaned for him.

* * * *

And then I was pumping Craig and Thorenson was pumping me. We were thrusting in unison, me into Craig and Craig back up at me, and Thorenson into me in rhythm with the increasing flashes of lightning and rolling of the thunder that now were nearly upon us. I gushed inside Craig's ass just as the deluge of the rain was let loose again.

Then Craig was gone, and I was in the middle of the bed, risen up on my shoulders, my pelvis straight up in the air, my white-socked legs wishboned out from my body, and Thorenson mounting me from above, holding my legs under the knees where the tops of the socks met them and thrusting down deeply into me, pumping me hard and fast from above. I watched our reflection in the window between the alternating bright flashes of lightning and dark of rainy night, my white-sheathed legs splayed in the air, the folds of a red plaid kilt spread out below me and on my belly. And in the reflection, beyond us, in the chair I had vacated, was the young actor, Craig, his legs now draped over the arms of the chair where I had sat, and his hand working inside what was left of the front of his white briefs. I cried out in ecstasy and passion as Thorenson pumped me. I was, of course, quite experienced in being taken, but the setting and the storm and the roaring fire and masterful cocksmanship of the Hollywood director—and, yes, the presence of his young protégé—were all highly arousing, and I arched my back and cried out in passion and came a second time as Thorenson unloaded deep inside me.

I spent the night in that big bed sandwiched between the director and the actor, the fire dying but never completely going out and the storm slowly subsiding. Sucking and being sucked; being side-split and side-splitting through the night. Moaning and causing moaning. Getting hard, ejaculating, going soft, getting hard, pumping, arousing and being aroused. And then, exhausted, sleeping, entwined and entwining.

I awoke between Thorenson and Craig. I kissed Craig on the lips and he sighed. And then as I carefully rose from between them, I leaned down and kissed Thorenson deeply as I worked his tool with my hand. He sighed in his sleep and quickly hardened. And as I rose from the bed, he and Craig rolled together and their lips met. When I came out of the bathroom, they were locked at the pelvis, Craig's lithe, hairless torso arched back to the side of the bed and his long leg draped over Thorenson's heavily muscled waist. Thorenson's long dong was three-quarters inside Craig's ass and was slowly churning in and out. Neither seemed to be fully awake, but both were moaning and sighing. I was sorely tempted to rejoin them.

I left the kilt and socks on the table and picked up my still-damp cowboy costume and forced my feet into the not-completely-dry boots. I dressed in my other clothes while standing beside the BMW and enjoying the fresh air that had come through with the storm and that, briefly, had pushed the smog of L.A. out over the ocean. I loved this town.

I briefly worried about missing my engagement down on Timberlake Drive the previous evening—but only briefly. If Freddie had had to take the call on his own, it served him right, and he might now think twice before doing it to me again. And if he'd bailed out, he would be the one in trouble, not me. I had $700 in my pocket and Freddie undoubtedly did not. Leon wouldn't care that I hadn't shown up—not when I flashed the money I had gotten here, which was more than I was supposed to have made in the original assignment. If Freddie hadn't shown or hadn't satisfied and the four guys complained, Leon would just tell them they needed to get the road names changed up here if they wanted to be found.

And I had found once again that my grandfather had been right. Always take the high road if given the choice. On my way down the mountain, I memorized how I had gotten here in the first place. I'd certainly come back if I could, and if I showed up on a rainy night in a kilt, I strongly suspect I would be welcomed appropriately. As I drove, I dreamed of maybe spinning this out to my chance in the movies.

Chapter 8: P.A. Club Night

"God, Leon. An M-8 special? Eight? I have to take eight of them in one gig? And what the hell is an Edwardian?" I knew what this was really about. I damn well knew that Leon was ticked because I had told him I was taking three months off, not to mention that I hadn't let him shag me yet.

"Hey, you're the one who told me in almost exactly the same breath that you were taking a whole chunk of time off but that you also needed a big-money assignment. Eight fucks in one night will be big bucks for you. And Edwardian would be Victorian era, like Lord Byron and Oscar Wilde. We've got stuff for that in the stockroom here—or near enough. You wouldn't likely be wearing it for very long anyway."

"But eight men in one night, Leon. Can't you . . . ?"

The voice on the phone went flat. Leon obviously wasn't the least bit interested in helping me out here. "Do you want the assignment or not?" he said in that "discussion closed" voice he used when the big gang bang assignments came in and had to be allotted to someone—usually to whoever he was irritated with that week. And the chief irritant obviously was me this week. I didn't have much leverage if I was planning to set the contract aside for a large chunk of time anyway. And I had no intention of telling him why I had to do that. I'm sure he wouldn't have approved of what I was going to do with the time.

"As I said, it's big bucks. We've got other studs here who would take it in heartbeat. But these guys asked for you specifically."

"Asked for me specifically?" I asked. Suddenly I was a little interested in this. "And so, if you give them what they want, it will be costing a bit more if it's really, really inconvenient for me to do the night?" I asked. "You'll pay me more than scale for this?"

Heavy breathing on the other end; Leon trying his best not to explode, maybe even popping a couple of those ulcer pills of his.

"Yes, of course, he said at last. A 25 percent bonus. I was going to tell you about that anyway, but you haven't given me a chance."

Sure, like hell you were going to do that for me, I thought to myself. But it was big bucks, and after you've had the first four cocks inside you in an evening, I guess cocks five through eight wouldn't mean much.

"So, who are these guys? And do they have a track record with us?" I asked. "And who gets off on a stripper dressed in stuffy old Victorian costume?"

"I don't know who they are," Leon answered. "This is the first time they've used us. As far as I can determine, it's some sort of small rich men's club that meets every couple of months. I guess they're bored with fucking each other and wanted a little spice in their lives."

I took the job, and beyond that initial whining—which we all did so management would know who was taking the brunt of this operation—I didn't let Leon know how angry I was that he had come to me with this assignment. I knew what this was all about. This was all about me taking three months off from their call boy stable. I knew I was one of their biggest money earners. And I knew they'd feel my absence in their pocketbooks too.

The costume looked good on me, even though it was too warm. The Edwardians were stuffy and so were their clothes. They seemed intent on covering everything in hot fabric, which wasn't anything like the amount of coverage male strippers usually had, even at the beginning of the gig. But the Edwardians seemed pretty much a contradiction, too. The costume was actually pretty sexy in its own way. I'd heard that the Victorians were stuffy on the surface but that they could be quite sensual people under all of that—and I knew that they had done some pretty wild partying in their era. This was borne out by what I had to wear.

The billowy white shirt, with a flamboyant red cravat thing at the neck, looked good on me, especially topped by the tight form-fitting vest. The coat over that was pretty bulky, but that would go as soon as I entered the door, I knew. But what really showed the interesting little contradictions of the Victorian era were the trousers. They were tight-legged and so tight in the crotch that you could see exactly which side my cock was dressed on and you could follow its entire length down toward the inside of my thigh. I told the dresser I thought I must have gotten trousers a couple of sizes too small, but he just snorted his prissy little snort and said this was exactly the way the Edwardians dressed, and that, in fact, Prince Albert, Queen Victoria's husband and the most Edwardian of the Edwardians, was well known for dressing down the left side contrary to the style of the time to dress down the right side. He apparently had the whole high society changing sides overnight, so whatever he was offering had to be readily apparent. Whatever, I thought this was a sexy idea that probably wasn't lost on the Victorians—apparently very modest dress, but putting the goods very much on display. I saw this as well in the bodice cleavage of those Victorian women who otherwise were buried in yards and yards of billowy material.

"A fashion revolution about where you put your cock and how you put it on display when you weren't fucking," I said. And then I laughed at my own joke, and the dresser laughed with me as he patted down my dressing to the left. He'd been trying to get my attention since I'd started working here. I wasn't interested, but at least it kept him laughing at my jokes. And he got a good feel off it, so we both left happy.

Later that evening, as I walked along Rodeo Drive in my Edwardian costume and with a shiny black beaver-skin top hat at a jaunty angle on my head, I decided this Victorian shit wasn't half bad. I was attracting a good bit of favorable attention, and if I'd left for the evening's work an hour or two earlier, I think I probably could have made a couple of hundred extra bucks in incidental blow jobs along the way—and that was on snooty Rodeo Drive.

I was surprised when I finally found the address I was looking for. There aren't that many of these old brick pile buildings left in downtown L.A., if indeed there ever had been many of them. I didn't know much about architecture, but if someone had given me a picture book and told me to pick out an Edwardian building, this one probably would have been my pick.

It wasn't a house, though, or even a gentleman's club, which is what I was sort of expecting. It was professional offices. And the address I was looking for proved to be a plush doctor's office that took up most of the building's second floor.

The place had good security. I had to stand out on the big porch on the front and ring the office. After a husky voice verified who I was, I was buzzed in. And then I had to repeat my litany of having been summoned here through a solid-looking door at the top of the main staircase and stand back for inspection through an eyehole.

When the door was opened, I immediately caught onto why they were so cautious about opening it up for just anyone. The man at the door—and all of the men I saw beyond that standing around in little groups with wine glasses and cigars—were stark naked. There were more than eight of them, which irritated me a little. I'd have to keep count while they were doing me so I'd know they weren't throwing a freebee in—and there was always the possibility that they would just force the extra dicking count. If so, I'd take it in my stride and keep count and take it up with Leon later. I'd learned that if you got too huffy about it, the situation might get a little dicey. Still, it was quite bothersome that there were more than eight of them.

The good news was that most of them were in fine shape, even though most of them appeared to be in their forties and fifties.

They welcomed me nicely and plied me with a glass of wine—well, several glasses of wine—and they didn't seem to be in any sort of rush for either a striptease or the gang fuck they had paid for.

We were in some sort of plush waiting room that was decorated more like a period parlor—like the building in a style I'd pick out as Victorian if I knew any more about furniture styles than I knew about architecture. One of the older men, very possibly the doctor whose name was on the door of this office suite, walked me around the room to show me off to his fellow club members.

In each group, I was engaged in some small talk—some really small talk; no one was revealing in any way who they were or what would make them stand out from any of the other nude men in the room. But in addition to the small talk, they were getting to know me a whole lot better. They were feeling me up, checking out the goods. And they were doing so as if this was the natural thing they all did at parties—get naked and all feel up the only dressed dude there. They were almost clinical about it, and the thought crossed my mind that maybe all of them were doctors.

But not all of them, I could see. My eye caught sight of a vaguely familiar blond hunk across the room who rang a bell at the base of my cock. This undoubtedly was why Leon had been asked for me specifically. The blond hunk had been the best man and an especially good swordsman at a B-6 Cowboy Special bachelors' party I had done a month or so earlier. He smiled and waved at me from across the room, confirming with the sloppy lustful grin he gave me that we, indeed, had met before. But he was a Mercedes salesman, I thought, not a doctor. And he also had a new toy between his legs he didn't have the last time we met. His newly acquired Prince Albert pierced cock toy was a shiny gold bar bell with big balls that matched the scale of his own.

While the other men crowded around me were talking

to me about nothing and running their hands down the inside thigh of my trousers to make sure I was "dressed" in the Prince Albert style, my mind was doing calculations on the name I had been given for their club and trying to figure out if that had a medical connection. But for the life of me, I couldn't put a definition to what a P.A. Club might be.

So I asked.

"Ah, the P.A. stands for Prince Albert," my doctor escort said in a matter-of-fact tone that indicated it wasn't a secret.

"Ah then, you're named for the Victorian period," I said. "You're all nineteenth-century England buffs." I almost choked on my own tongue, though, when I realized I had used the word "buff" in a roomful of naked men.

"Not precisely," the doctor said. "We're actually named for this." And as he said that, he took his very presentable cock in his hand and waved it at me.

And then I saw it. I don't know why I didn't focus on it as soon as I'd walked into the room. The men weren't completely naked at all. They all had something in common. All of them had jewelry things poking out of their dick heads. Some were open loops with rounded beads where the loops stopped, some closed loops, some looked like miniature barbells, and some were studs made out of various things: gold or silver cubes or knobs or gem stones. One of the younger, studlier guys had a loop with what looked like a ruby heart charm hanging off it.

"These are Prince Alberts," the doctor was saying. "The members of our club all have them. This is our annual initiation meeting. We'll initiate a new member tonight. Prince Albert was said to have originated this idea for Victorian gentleman and to have had one himself. His name stuck on penis piercing."

Fascinating, I thought, about the Prince Albert jewelry. Absolutely fascinating. Who would have thought it of the husband of the stuffy old Queen Victoria? Those Victorians. Gotta love 'em. They had us fooled about them being so uptight. And, of course, a doctor's office would be a natural place for a party like this.

As the evening wore on, the club members became friendlier to me and friskier with their hands—and some with their lips—and increasingly helpful in equalizing our circumstances by slowly helping me off with my hot clothes. And I became more and more taken with the good wine they were sharing around.

I began to earn my fee in earnest. The party spread out from the waiting room into the examination rooms, and the club members were becoming as friendly and frisky with each other as they were with me. They were pairing off in couples and threesomes, and a few of them were disappearing into the area of the examination rooms. But a few of them were also fucking right there in the waiting room, on the floor, in the chairs, and on the reception desk. That was fine with me. Maybe it meant that all but eight of them would wear each other out before they got around to me.

The doctor and a few of the other members, the younger ones, I was happy to note, guided me through a door and toward the back of the building. As we passed doors, I could see that the smaller groups that had come this way earlier were having no trouble amusing themselves with the medical equipment and with each other in the examination rooms branching off from the hallway.

I was quite woozy from the wine at this point, but it was time for me to start keeping count. I was down to just the billowy shirt, which was fully open, and that silk red cravat around my neck. Several of the men had me backed up to an examination table and were running their hands and lips all over my body. My doctor escort left briefly but came back with a box full of condoms and a bottle of what must be lubricant. As my first customer, a short blond guy with a short, but fat cock, was kneeling on the examination table, with me facing him and him using my mouth to get his cock as pumped up as it was going to get, the doctor escort was rubbing the lubricant into my hole and on my cock as well.

He told me the lubricant would help me take several men easier and that I would feel a bit numb after only a few

79

minutes, but that this would keep me from tightening up. He was very clinical in his explanation.

The table was really too high for the little blond to do anything to me, so when he came off the table, he pulled me over to a chair, sat in it, and pulled me down on his lap, facing the other men, and made me fuck myself on his cock while the other men gathered around, licking their lips, stroking themselves, and waiting their turn. I felt his Prince Albert, a gold cube, rubbing along the side of my passage as he stroked me. Very intriguing. In fact I could feel all of the different Prince Alberts—and in different ways—that I took that evening. They were truly awesome toys, and I wondered briefly if Queen Victoria cried out with passion as I did for the little blond and all his successors when Prince Albert played her with one of those. They certainly did it often enough, as attested by her large stable of offspring.

The next man, a tall, thin redhead with a long, slender cock to match, had me kneel in the chair, facing the back, and he fucked me from the rear, taking long strokes into me that were quite pleasant, really. He was good about putting his hands under my shirt and onto my chest and tweaking my nipples in rhythm with his fuck. He had one of those upturned cocks and had a Prince Albert that was an open ring with two big silver knobs. They dragged in unison across my upper canal walls as he fucked me, and I rewarded his efforts and those talented silver balls with my first ejaculation of the evening to the delight and encouragement of a very attentive audience.

Then I was taken from behind by number three while I was standing on the floor and my chest was pressed to the top of the examination table and my mouth was working black and curly-haired number four's plump cock. Number four's Prince Albert was like a bar bell, so my passage walls got extra loving on both sides as he slid in and out of me. He wanted to cuddle close in behind me and kiss me on the neck as he was stroking, and I found that curly haired chest of his rubbing up and down on my back as he fucked quite arousing and satisfying.

Number five wanted me on the floor beside the table, me on my back, and him holding my pelvis up and my legs out and pumping me fast and furiously while his teeth worked my nipples. His cocksmanship was especially inventive, and I arched my back and thrust my pelvis up into his as his Prince Albert found and kissed every square inch of my insides. Number six liked that position as well, but he had me on the top of the examination table. He was the hunk with the heart-shaped pendant on his Prince Albert loop, and he was quite pleased that I wanted to closely watch that disappear into and emerge from my hole while he plowed me. I erupted and flowed for him. Number seven just flipped me over onto my stomach and covered me close with his arms and torso, told me to come up a bit on my knees, and slowly pumped me with the longest and fattest cock I'd had yet that evening. He took his time and had me moaning and groaning for it. I had felt the distinct Prince Albert feature of all them as they dicked me— and I loved the feel of what they all had, but this seventh miner had the biggest, thickest ring of all on his longest and thickest cock. And he had attached a string of beads to the ring. These were swirling around inside me while he fucked me, and they sent me straight to bottom heaven.

I'm not sure that there was a number eight—and for all I was able to be aware of at the time, there might have been a number twelve and thirteen as well. Number seven had me royally fucked and the wine had me woozy as hell, and that lubricant had me numb on the surface, if not inside my canal.

I was aware of a muscle-bound bald guy sitting on my chest with me stretched out on the examination table on my back. I had some impression that my wrists and ankles were bound to the table, but I was too far gone to be sure of that. The bald guy was feeding me with his cock, fucking my face and making me suck him, while he held my head very still between two beefy palms. Many men—it seemed like the full contingent of men who had been at the party to begin with— were gathered around the table and ooing and ahing and making small talk to each other in whispers. I saw the escort doctor, a blur of white now, no longer naked, come around below me, and I felt him thrust inside me with his crowned cock. He had a fist wrapped around my cock as he fucked me, but my cock was so numb that I couldn't be sure of that. After some deep stroking, the doctor just held himself deep inside me, very still. The bald guy on top of me kept holding my head still with his hands and feeding my mouth with his hard cock. He was cooing to me, whispering words of encouragement for I know not what—nor did I really care at the moment; I was well-gone drunk and very well fucked.

For a short time, the room was swathed in an eerie silence. And then there was a buzzing of voices and some healthy applause sweeping around the room, and the party seemed to be taking off for a second round of frivolity.

The room nearly emptied out, and I found I was pulling myself up to a seated position on the table and rubbing my wrists as if they had, indeed, been bound. The bald guy was gone as well. Only my doctor escort remained, and he was decked out in a white surgical costume now and had a white gauze cup over his mouth.

He removed the face mask and gave me the broadest of smiles and said, "Welcome to the club."

I looked down, and there it was. I had a thickish loop pierced through my mushroom cap. It was gold and it had a gold bead on it.

I had been initiated, crowned, pierced, made a colleague of Prince Albert. I celebrated by rolling my eyes up into my head and falling back onto the surface of the examination table and passing out.

For days thereafter, Leon wouldn't take my telephone calls. I did, however, receive a hefty check in the mail for the evening's work, and I'd received a nice fat tip from the guys in the P.A. Club as well—although there was no reason for Leon ever to know that.

I'm sure he figured that I was, by right, totally pissed with him and might do him bodily harm if I caught up with him before the post-surgical pain wore off. I'm sure, though, that he also was crowing to himself that he had punished me for wanting to take three months off, especially since someone had to take this eight-male-fucks assignment—the payoff was much too good to turn it down—and anyone who did would be out of commission, recovering from the surgery, for three months.

* * * *

I'd been told to avoid sex for three months, the exact time I had said I needed to take off. Which meant I wasn't trying to contact Leon to ream him a new one; I was trying to call him to gloat. I was taking the three months because I had decided I wanted my dick head pierced and a nice gold loop put in it, although I had no idea at the time that it was called a Prince Albert. Before this assignment came along, I would have had to swallow the cost of both the surgery and the recovery myself. Thanks to the P.A. Club, however, I'd now gotten that all for free—along with a club membership, membership in a club that included a master fucker number seven with a mean string of ass canal beads.

Chapter 9: Triple Magnum Nabilum

I had to turn my eyes away from the penetrating stare of Finn Bergstrum, so I took my first good look at his assistant, Nabil. "Satyr" was the first thought that entered my mind, and I almost was able to imagine two little horns above his ears there. Sharp, swarthy features with that almost sneer of a smile that was close to the edge of presumption and cruelty without losing an ability to claim interest and encouragement, if challenged. Jet black hair and eyes, and that pointed goatee that accentuated the struggle between sensitivity and raw animalism. The struggle accentuated by the hand that reached out for his wine glass: Long, sensuous artist's finger, but curly black hair on the back of the hand down to his knuckles. He was giving me a proprietary look— which, of course, was his privilege. I'd been bought and paid for to be here.

I looked back at Bergstrum, embarrassed at the feeling that I was distinctly out of my depth and perhaps even out of my league, and further embarrassed that anything like this could ever embarrass me after what I'd seen in this business. When Leon had set this up and handed me the air tickets, he only said that this was a very special corporate arrangement, that I'd been very lucky to be selected, and that I should be very accommodating. From the amount on the accompanying check, I decided that, indeed, I could be very accommodating. I'd flown to Zurich, checked in by prior arrangement at the Hotel Softel, and had barely slept for five hours before I was called down to the hotel's intimate and heavily masculine "gentlemen's" bar.

I had known the name Finn Bergstrum even before being handed the assignment. Who hadn't heard of it? Entrepreneur on the grand scale. Instant relief to corporations in the need of being saved and even more immediate panic in the halls of corporations rumored to have been added to his takeover lists. Reclusive, eccentric, somewhere just short of God, the tabloids said. And whispers about his sexual tastes and capabilities as well—at least in the pools in which I swam. Well, I'd just met him, and already I was trembling. This didn't normally happen to me.

He was ugly as sin, a regular gargoyle. But when I looked back at him, here in the Softel Hotel's dimly lit gentlemen's bar, I was overwhelmed by his presence and the raw power he exuded. He could have tipped me over this table right here, stripped me, and plowed me in front of all of the sedate bankers and brokers sitting around us sipping their martinis and smoking their Cuban cigars and I would have moaned and moved my hips for him, glad that he had selected me.

Craggy features, chiseled in a Mount Everest rawness and a powerful body, barely contained by a tailored silk tuxedo—heavy but obviously built for stamina and speed, the muscled presence of a bison. He filled the room; he owned the room. Strong hands the size of hubcaps and thick, gnarly fingers that set my butt atwitching.

There was no doubt why I was here, what I was supposed to do for him. This is what I did. I'd been told the bare facts of the deal. He'd agreed not to take over a major U.S. corporation for certain remunerations and accommodations. I—or someone like me—was just one of the accommodations. Just for one night. All the way from New York to Zurich just for one night. What I'd found in my paycheck was more than enough to cover anything that would happen in that one night.

I'd done this before—if, certainly, not on this scale.

"So, is all understood, Mr. Smith?" Bergstrum asked me, as he took a long, thin cigar out of his mouth and tapped its ash head carefully in a silver-lined wooden tray. As he did so, I noticed three silver boxes, of varying lengths and widths, laying on the surface of the cocktail table between us.

His milky blue eyes, peeking out from under bushy silver-gray eyebrows, pierced me, and I looked away quickly, down to his hand, resting atop the stack of boxes. Those thick fingers. My butt twitched again. Projecting ahead. Trying to remember whether I'd heard anything specific from the rumors about his proclivities.

"Yes, certainly," I answered. "I am ticketed for an early morning flight. I assume—"

"Of course I know your flight schedule, Mr. Smith," Bergstrum said, overriding my sentence.

"Then—," I started to say, indicating that I was quite prepared to vacate the bar and get on with the evening.

"Oh, do finish your drink, Mr. Smith," Bergstrum said. "I don't think that Nabil here has finished admiring you yet. And what do you think of my assistant, Nabil, Mr. Smith? Do you find him . . . suitable?"

"Ummm. Yes, of course," I stammered. What in the hell did that mean, I wondered.

"Nabil, here, is my right-hand man, Mr. Smith. My hands and eyes and my ears and my . . . well, let's just say all of my appendages."

Well, Hokay, I thought. But I wasn't being paid to be confused or smart. So I turned my face toward Nabil and gave him a friendly smile. He gave me back a smart-assed look fully conveying that this night would be a double. Well, that was OK, too. That was no surprise. I couldn't shake the satyr image that pinged at my brain every time I looked at him. He wasn't tall or thin, but he was strongly built. I gauged him to be Turkish probably. Some Mediterranean blend certainly. Somewhat of a surprise set off against the hulking Norwegian. And much younger than Bergstrum. The image of the two of them fucking flashed through my mind. This was immediately followed by the vision of the two of them fucking me, and my hand trembled a little. Nabil would be nothing new, other than that satyrish puckishness about him. But Bergstrum. I just didn't know. I didn't usually lose control on the job, and he was such an ugly lump. But there was something about him that had me off balance. Those fingers. I looked at them again. Strong, thick. I couldn't help but thinking of—

"Three boxes, Mr. Smith." Bergstrum was holding up the top, squarish silver box over the table between us. "Perhaps you can give us some idea of your preference."

He flipped open the lid of the box away from me. Cigars. Five cigars, of varying brands laid out in a row, snuggled into red velvet as if they were the crown jewels—and, although I knew next to nothing about cigars, I had no doubt that these cigars were as preciously bought as crown jewels.

"Oh, no thank you," I said. "I don't smoke. Thanks anyway."

"Oh, these aren't for smoking, Mr. Smith." He paused and gave me a broad, friendly smile. I turned to Nabil; he gave me a leery grin.

"Let me tell you how we rate cigars," Bergstrum continued after that pregnant pause. "First, by length. All of these in this box are six inches or less in length. Sort of the standard size; but maybe a bit long . . . for a cigar." He gave me a piercing look; gauging whether I was following his meaning. I wasn't a dummy; I understood we weren't talking about cigars.

"The other rating is in girth, diameter, if you will, Mr. Smith. We call this rating ring gauge. A sixty-four ring gauge would be equal to an inch. The cigars in this box all range around fifty ring gauge. Again, a bit thick for a cigar . . . if perhaps a somewhat disappointing thickness for, well, you know."

Yes, I did know.

"But we have several cigars here," Bergstrum said, and he flashed me a broad smile.

"So," he continued, "there are some very nice cigars in this case. Indian Tabac Cameroon Legenda Gorilla— interesting name, wouldn't you say? At six inches in length and a fifty-eight ring gauge, it's quite a formidable cigar, as cigars go. Or perhaps one of my favorites; this is a La Gloria Cubana Series R., No. 6, which is slightly shorter at five and seven-eighths inches, but a bit thicker at a sixty ring gauge. Do these interest you, Mr. Smith, or would you like to see what is in the second box before noting a preference?"

"Oh, let's look in the second box," I said. Obviously I'd said the right thing, as both Bergstrum and Nabil gave me approving looks.

"You'll notice this box is longer than the first one, Mr. Smith," Bergstrum said in hushed tones. "These are the truly extraordinary gems of the cigar world." He took up the second box and flipped it open. Surprise. More cigars. Longer and thicker than those in box number one. Same silver encasing, blue velvet lining this time.

I could tell these were special to Bergstrum. He lifted them out one at a time, his hands trembling a bit. Those thick fingers lovingly handling the cigars. I could feel the heat rising in me. This was unusual for me. Bergstrum had something in him that aroused me. I had little question why he was so successful in the business world. Most probably called it charisma. I had other names for it.

"We are into the longer beauties now, Mr. Smith. Very few exist at this level. The Casa Blanca Magnum, at seven inches and a ring gauge of sixty is lovely, don't you think? Or this Padron Magnum Maduro at a full nine inches, fifty ring gauge." He was expecting me to be impressed, and I was impressed. I was being well paid to be impressed. I would have been less impressed if we were really talking about cigars, but, of course, we weren't.

"Now we could improve upon those, but we'd have to make choices." Bergstrum was continuing on. At this point I don't think he even needed me in the room. Nabil was sitting closer to Bergstrum now, and he was looking intently, worshipfully at the older man. And he had a hand on Bergstrum's inner thigh. This was obviously something of a precoital ceremony for the two of them. I said nothing. My paycheck was already banked.

"For length, you might like the Perfecxion A Giant, at nine and a quarter inches, but only a forty-seven ring gauge. And if your preference went to thickness, here's a Special Jamaican Rey Del Rey, at nine inches, but with a ring gauge of sixty. What do you think, Mr. Smith? Are these interesting to you, or should we perhaps go back to the first box?" Bergstrum's voice was rasping now. Nabil's hand had found his basket and was gently massaging it.

"No, this box is fine," I said, trying my best to match Bergstrum's rasping voice and to show him lustful eyes. He was clearly pleased. And I'll have to admit that the lustful eyes required no acting. Nabil's other hand was on my basket now, and I was showing him that I, indeed, was following along with this game.

"Then just maybe you might be interested in the actor Orson Welles's favorite, Mr. Smith?"

"Yes, I was wondering about that one," I said in a breathy voice, having had my eye on the last cigar in the box ever since Bergstrum had opened it. If Nabil didn't stop his attentions, I might come right here in the gentlemen's bar. I could see by the way he'd tented up Bergstrum's pants that I hadn't been mistaken about those chunky fingers of his.

"This is a Casa Blanca Jeroboam," Bergstrum said, his voice full of wonder. "Orson Welles's cigar of choice. Ten inches long and a sixty-six ring gauge."

We all sat there for a moment, drinking in the size of that humongous cigar. Nabil was still stroking Bergstrum's crotch, but he had abandoned mine for his own.

"Would you like to make choices for Nabil and me, Mr. Smith?"

I contemplated the pickings for a few brief moments, wondering what would be most acceptable. "How about the Perfecxion A Giant for Nabil?" I said.

"And for me?" Bergstrum's eyes were slitted and his chest was heaving up and down from the attention Nabil was giving him.

"The Casa Blanca Jeroboam, of course," I said.

That had been the right answer, obviously. But I

pressed on. "But what about the third box?" I asked. I could see it was longer than the other two, although much narrower.

"Ah, that would be the Triple Magnum Nabilum," Bergstrum said. "Perhaps later." Both Bergstrum and his assistant were struggling up out of their plush club chairs at that point.

* * * *

Bergstrum's room at the Softel, or rooms, I should say, were about twelve times larger than the accommodations I had been given. And they were about four degrees plusher, even though, had I not seen Bergstrum's digs, I would have assumed that I'd been given the best accommodations in the hotel.

But I didn't really see much of the room. As far as the decor went, my eyes were mainly on the edge of the canopy over Bergstrum's massive bed. I was on my back at the edge of the bed, holding my thighs up and out, and Bergstrum was hunched between them and working my ass canal with the Perfecxion A. Giant cigar I'd selected for Nabil, while Nabil was over to the side, clearly in my vision, stripping down.

The cigar was somewhat of a surprise; the foreplay down in the gentlemen's bar hadn't been as symbolic as I had imagined it would be. I really was being fucked by an expensive nine and a half-inch cigar. But in my line of business and at the prices I commanded, this wasn't as surprising as some other moments in my life had been.

Nabil was much more of a surprise. The satyr impression held true. His dark-skinned well-muscled torso was smooth skin down to the waist, with the exception of patches of black curly hair around his ring-pierced nipples, but when he stripped his tuxedo pants off, I could hardly tell he'd done so. From the waist down, he was covered in thick, curly black hair that looked almost like a pelt. His forearms were equally hirsute. If he'd had cloven feet, I would have sworn he was a true satyr. As it was, he certainly was horse hung.

Leaving the Perfecxion A Giant buried in my ass, Bergstrum moved back to the other side of me from where

91

Nabil had stripped and sank into a chair, still well within my line of vision. Nabil cantered up to him and Bergstrum took Nabil's cock in his mouth and worked it up. After only a few moments, however, Nabil walked back over to me and retrieved the cigar. He went to a side table, put the cigar in his mouth, struck a match to the tip of the cigar, and took a few puffs. Then he returned to Bergstrum, stuck the cigar in Bergstrum's mouth, sank down to his knees between Bergstrum's thighs, unzipped the hulking Norwegian's tux fly, and fed on the huge piece of meat he found there. Bergstrum let his head loll back on the top of the chair and hummed and puffed on the cigar. After a bit, he groaned and lurched, and I could tell he had come.

He picked up box number two from a table beside the chair and handed Nabil the Casa Blanca Jeroboam cigar. Nabil approached me between my now-relaxed legs, lifted my legs up and out, and made clear I was to hold my own legs up myself, which I did—ever mindful of what I was being paid for this— while he fucked me with the thicker and longer Casa Blanca Jeroboam.

Bergstrum sat in his chair, legs thrown out, cigar puffing, and a beefy hand stroking his own cock back to life as he watched Nabil slowly, and inventively, work my ass canal with the Casa Blanca Jeroboam. At length, Bergstrum gave a hoarse cough, lurched up from his chair, and joined Nabil between my legs. He forced the wet end of the Perfecxion alongside the Casa Blanca Jeroboam inside me, and I now was being fucked more fully and quite deeply with two counterpistoning cylinders of expensive tobacco. Nabil was working my nipples with his free hand and Bergstrum was stroking my cock. They also were doing a good lip lock on each other. Those strong, beefy fingers of Bergstrum's were wrapped around my cock and stroking it. Oh, Gawd. And they continued this until I ejaculated.

Then it was Bergstrum back in his chair, with Nabil kneeling between his thighs and giving him another blow job.

"You asked about the third box, Mr. Smith," Bergstrum called over to me. "About the Triple Magnum

Nabilum."

"Umm, umm," I replied. Still mellow after my meltdown.

He lifted and opened the third box, which had been lying under box number two on the table. He turned and showed me the contents of the box.

Surprise. Yet another cigar. But, carumba, what a cigar.

"Ten and a half inches long, 120 ring gauge. Almost not big enough to get in my mouth, Mr. Smith. I have these made especially for me. And do you know where the name came from, Mr. Smith?"

"Umm, umm," I repeated.

"Triple Magnum Nabilum, Mr. Smith. Nabilum. From Nabil, Mr. Smith. Our own Nabil here provided the specifications for them, Mr. Smith."

"Umm, umm," I managed.

"And now I smoke this, Mr. Smith . . . while you smoke Nabil."

Oh.

While I watched Bergstrum lean back in his chair, legs thrown out, mouth puffing his huge Triple Magum Nabilum, and his hand stroking his cock, he watched me, first, try to manage Nabil's cock in my mouth, which was no small feat. Then he sat back, with his hand on his own tool, dozing from time to time, and watched an ever-alert Nabil fuck me with his ten-and a half-inch long, two-inch-in-diameter cock through much of the rest of the night, with Nabil showing that he could stay hard through wave after wave of ejaculations.

Despite all of my professional training, I cried out at the first entry, and moaned and groaned and bunched up clumps of satin bedspread in my fists and did what I could not to bite off my tongue as a sneering satyr of prodigious proportions and inhuman staying power fucked me to his completion. The satyr image kept floating up, as our hips swung back and forth, my legs wrapped around his waist and my hands gripping the heavy pelting of his bulbous buttocks and heavily muscled thighs. I had been trained to please a man, and I could tell that Nabil was beside himself with lust to be drawn as far as he could inside me and to explore every nook and cranny of my channel. As he was about to pull out of me for his first shooting, I contracted my canal closely around his sword and held him inside me, riding his pelvis hard as he twitched and then lurched again and again and again. A series of little cries from the direction of Bergstrum's chair gave evidence that he was joining us in release.

After ejaculating, Nabil brought his mouth down onto my nipples and ravished them while he stroked me to another flowing. Then he turned me belly down on the bed and fucked me again to ejaculation and then turned me and dug in even deeper and stretched me even wider, with Bergstrum puffing on his Triple Magnum Nabilum and coming in consort with Nabil's spoutings as if they practiced this every night.

Bergstrum had just paid for that one night, but, with Nabil's help, he got his full money's worth. I was fucked into the dawn, and could hardly stand or walk straight when the two men were finally done with me.

On the plane trip home the next morning, as the soreness of my body and my inability to close my legs made me ever grateful for the first-class ticket, my one regret was that Bergstrum hadn't fucked me. I left aching for that. That was the power he had.

Maybe next time.

Chapter 10: Saddled

I was immediately suspicious. Leon was smiling today and talking nice. Just yesterday he'd propositioned me for the hundredth time and I'd turned him down for the hundredth and one times—I'd turned him down before he asked the first time. The most recent time I'd turned him down he'd gotten pissy, I'd given him lip back, and he'd pulled back a lucrative assignment—for a faded, and largely harmless, movie star gig that would have paid my rent for the rest of the month.

And yet he'd called me in again today. Usually after one of these fights with my pimp—for that's what I now called Leon out of resignation—I would be left in limbo for a week or more. I decided he must be short of staff.

"You ride a horse, don't you?" he asked, using his fat lips to shift his smoldering cigar from one cheek to the other.

"Yes, of course," I answered, thinking that maybe that's what narrowed down the pickings to me.

"Thought so. Pack your bags for the weekend." And, with that, Leon slapped an airplane ticket folder down on the coffee table. I picked it up. Destination Dulles Airport, the international airport located in northern Virginia that serviced the Washington, D.C., area.

"Where from there?" I asked.

"You'll be picked up. Client doesn't want to say."

"And the driver will know me by . . .?"

"Oh, yeah, you'll be a platinum blond." Leon was smiling. I didn't think this was all he had to say. But I stood and turned for the door. If I had to dye my hair before I had to be at the airport, I'd best get to it.

"All over." Leon said. I turned, and he was grinning. Well, OK, that made sense if the hair color was a fetish of the client's. More time, though. Still Leon seemed entirely too pleased. I stood there, knowing I hadn't heard it all yet.

"Except, there is to be little all over. You're to shave everything but your head and a V at the bush."

"A V at the bush," I said in a deadpanned voice.

"Yes, pointing to the goods."

"Well, OK, I've had to do worse," I said. I took one last look at Leon before I turned and left the room. He still had a sloppy grin on his face. I still had the uneasy feeling that I didn't know everything he found amusing. But it wasn't my job to know everything. I got paid very well for doing what I did and shutting up about it.

My plane was two hours late landing at Dulles, apparently because bad weather at both the Chicago and Atlanta airports, which were nowhere near where I was traveling, had the jets stacked up in holding patterns across the country. I didn't mind the extra time in the air, though. Our flight wasn't crowded, and I made friends with a distinguished-looking man sitting beside me who I'm sure I recognized from the television as in some sort of political job. We had enough time to chat that the delay earned me an extra $100, when I let him slip into one of the johns with me and give me a blow job, him sitting on the can beating his meat into a paper hand towel and me with my butt perched on the small sink and my heels dug into the rubber-matted floor to counteract the slight pitching of the plane. He seemed turned on by the platinum-blond V and licked it down into swirls of curly waves, so I guess that wasn't such a bad idea after all.

I hadn't been standing at the baggage area for long—I didn't have more than I could put in my carry-on, but this was where I was told to stand—before I was approached by an extremely well-turned-out coffee with cream young guy, complete with contrasting dark brown chauffeur's livery and a big welcoming smile on his face. He was maybe three or four years younger than I was and shorter than I was by a couple of inches. He was a little stocky—but in a solid, four hours-a-day in the gym sort of way. Bullet headed, totally bald, big hands, big feet in his slicked-up black shiny shoes. All promising.

He seemed to have no question who I was. I was standing in front of the designated pillar just off to the left of the baggage belt—and there was the platinum hair that I had moussed up into slight spikes. The West Coast surfer look to go with the tan I'd worked so hard on. I struck the pose for him, and I could tell in an instant he was interested. I often found the clients barely fuckable, but I occasionally, like now, was able to develop other side prospects while on a job. That gym-muscled look, the big hands and the big feet. And the bald head. Testosterone building up somewhere.

He took my bag, even though we both knew I could handle it without any huffing, and led me up the ramp to where a black Lincoln limo was parked right at the door, its engine idling, daring an airport cop to give it a ticket and find out who he or she had inconvenienced.

Eric wasn't exactly chatty, but he willingly gave me his name as we nosed out of the airport spaghetti pattern of roads and onto Route 28—at least according to the signs—and headed east toward I-95, the main highway running north and south on the East Coast. He didn't ask me my name, however, and he shut down when I asked him the name of the one who had sent for me. Good. Eric didn't fuck and tell.

When he turned west on Route 50 before we got to the intersection with I-95, he was friendly enough to tell me where we were going.

"Middleburg. We'll still be in this suburban congestion for a while, but it won't be much more than half an hour now before we reach Middleburg. Five Oaks. It's just on the other side of Middleburg."

Ah, information. I liked to have my bearings. At least

something to process if a client was being too rough and I wanted to head for the exit.

"Middleburg. Middleburg. I've heard of that before, but I don't—"

"Maybe from back in the Kennedy era," Eric said. He had his eyes looking at me in the rearview mirror. He looked very interested. He obviously had been told not to say much, but he wanted to be friendly. He was assessing me just like I was assessing him.

"You may be too young," he continued, "but you may have heard about Jackie Kennedy and her horse riding both when her husband was president and then for years later. They had a retreat out here in Middleburg. They ride to the hounds out here, old southern style. The closest place to the White House that she could do that."

Ah, yes, I remembered hearing that now. Horse riding. Another piece of the puzzle Leon had tossed out on the coffee table. I was riding to the hounds this weekend, maybe. I wondered if Leon had any idea what the difference was between western saddle riding in California canyons and riding to the hounds in Virginia. Well, I'd cope. I always did.

"Thanks, Eric," I said. "Thanks for the information."

"Don't mention it." He was giving me a big smile in the mirror. Some sort of understanding established. I had a friend here if I needed it—maybe a very friendly friend. I took the plunge.

"Later, maybe, Dude?" I said and flashed him a smile.

"I'd like that," Eric answered, the grin I could see in the rearview mirror going from ear to ear.

After driving through Middleburg, one of those "quaint" little country towns that looked like it had barely cleared the eighteenth century and was obviously dripping in old money, we drove for maybe six more miles. The scenery was quite an attractive and calming switch from the frenetic pace and arid conditions I'd left that morning—rolling Virginia countryside of majestic oak trees, well-trimmed pasture land, and endless sweeps of white-painted wood rail fencing set against the backdrop of bluish-shaded mountains to the west.

We turned off to the south and drove not more than a half mile more before we turned right between two massive stone columns with marble eagles perched on top of each. A bronze plaque in one of the columns announced we were at Five Oaks.

"The original five oaks are all gone now, but a lot more have been planted," Eric suddenly piped up from the front seat. He hadn't spoken since we'd struck our unspoken deal. We'd both been sitting and enjoying the scenery—and at least I was contemplating what Eric had to offer under that dark brown chauffeur's livery.

I grunted my acknowledgment that I'd heard what he said and appreciated the bit of conversation. He went on, "There are more like a hundred oaks now. Northern money."

Another piece of proffered information. A client who was rich and on the make in the South while being carpetbagger. Grasping and probably anger issues. I sensed bondage and maybe a bit of SM. Well, with the fees we charged, we did see a bit of that. Leon knew I had my limits. But maybe that was why Leon was so nice all of a sudden after our fight and had that sloppy grin on his face when we parted. Maybe he knew my limits were going to be challenged.

We drove for maybe another quarter mile on a freshly asphalted two-lane road running between some or all of those hundred oaks, which must have been pretty mature when they were planted, because they were quite impressive now.

I heard where we were headed before I saw it. The baying of hounds. We turned a corner and there it was, a massive, stately brick building, a traditional American Georgian four over four over an English basement with wide portico held up by four hefty white columns. Newer, but still old, two-story brick wings jutted out from either flank of the antebellum center structure. And gathered on an oval lawn in front of the house was a swirl of sleek, lean horses; equally sleek riders in scarlet coats and tan breeches; and an undercurrent of teeming lean hounds, some black, some brown, but most white with brown splotches on them. Everything was chaos and loud gossiping and obvious preparation for a fox hunt. I thought I'd stumbled onto an MGM set. I expected to see Elizabeth Taylor and Rock Hudson stride down the stairs from the portico and mount their fine fillies at any moment.

I had only a glimpse of this, though, as Eric pulled the limo around the side of the house and wound his way through a sea of Mercedes and Jaguars and BMWs, many with horse trailers attached, all parked willy-nilly around under the trees at the side and back of the house. Eric pulled up to a detached five-car garage, hidden neatly behind huge boxwoods at the back corner of the house. He retrieved my bag from the trunk and ushered me, without a word, as if he sensed we now were being closely monitored, into a side door of the house.

We were in a narrow, oriental-carpeted hallway that split the width of the house. From down the hall, I glimpsed a distant patch of light, and from that direction I could hear loud conversation and the braying of a loud voice for someone to get out there and get the hunt in order. We continued walking toward the voice and light and eventually arrived in the broad center hallway of the center structure.

The braying voice belonged to a distinguished-looking, trim, yet solidly built, handsome in a matured way man, with carefully barbered hair with gray sweeps at the temples, standing at the foot of a sweeping curved staircase rising to the upper story, several paces short of a double door with wide side windows looking out onto the portico. The doors were open, and I once again saw beyond those the swirl of scarlet jackets and fine horse flesh standing in a frenetic swirl of braying hounds. The man, who obviously was in charge— who obviously was in charge no matter where he was— was alone in the foyer by the time Eric and I reached it. He turned and saw us and scowled.

"You're late," he said. "Almost missed it. Eric take him to the scarlet room. Dress quickly and come down. We have a horse ready for you. You should be able to make the last trumpet."

That was it. That was all he said, and then he was out the door. I didn't have much doubt this was the client and that he was the dominating type.

We started up the stairs, Eric ushering me to go first. Half way up we were accosted by another equestrian hurrying down the stairs, pulling on white kid gloves, decked out like the rest, a black velvet-covered helmet already on his head.

The same man who had just walked out the front door onto the portico.

"You're late," he said in the same disapproving, "to-be-obeyed" voice. "Dress quickly and get out there." He swept by me, brushing against my sleeve. Eric, probably well accustomed to this, deftly turned to let him pass without contact.

Twins. There were two of them. Identical twins. Another possible explanation for Leon's grin.

Eric escorted me up the stairs and down a long transverse hallway deep into one of the wings. The silence of the house contrasted with the muted sound of the developing hunt filtering through thick brick walls. He stopped at the last door on the right down the hall at the back of the house, opened the door, and set my carry-on inside. Then he stepped back to let me enter. When I had moved through the door, I heard him say, "I wouldn't be long changing, if I were you," the door clicked behind me, and I was alone.

Scarlet was a good name for the room. It certainly was scarlet—the carpet, the drapes on the windows, the bedspread and drapery on the solid mahogany four-poster canopy bed set between two windows looking into the back yard. The spines on the books in the bookcases beside the fireplace. A rich-looking Bergama oriental rug spread in front of the fireplace had a scarlet background. Even the burnished wood of the walls as well as the fireplace mantel and surround were a rich red mahogany.

I could see riding clothes laid out on the bed and a pair of gleaming black leather riding boots at the foot of the bed, with a black leather riding crop balanced on the toes. A riding shirt, a scarlet jacket, a black velvet-covered riding helmet, and a pair of tan breeches that flared at the hips and had leather ovals at the inner thighs—the three-quarter-length breeches that were called jodhpurs. And an athletic supporter with a sturdy cup made out of some sort of hard plastic.

I walked over to the foot of the bed and looked up into the canopy frame. Just as I thought. A steel-cage structure inside the wooden frame that gave the bed stability and would take a lot of weight. And in the upper corners at the top of the pillars at the foot of the bed, leather leads and ankle restraints tucked up into the canopy. I walked around to the head of the bed as I started shedding my clothes. I saw the black leather bands around slats at the headboard and looked between the headboard and the wall. Sure enough, wrist restraints tucked down there.

Despite the initial impression of pristine polish, I could see gouges and minute scruff marks on the woodwork that indicated a strenuous workout in the past of the restraints. They weren't just for "what if?" contingencies.

I opened the door of the nightstand beside the bed. Piles of condoms, tubes of lube, a collection of dildos, leather blindfolds, and gags with rubber balls for the mouth to prevent the subject from biting his tongue or pulverizing his teeth by gnashing them.

Scarlet room. A very good name for it. Well, forewarned and all that. At least the fee was appropriately impressive.

I dressed quickly, and all fit well—Leon obviously having given them my measurements—except that the jodhpurs were skin tight. They were so low slung the top of my platinum V spilled out in curls over the waistband that were quite noticeable before I got the shirt and jacket on, and I wasn't so sure that the seams of the jodhpurs would hold under the strain of my thighs and glutes.

The hunt wasn't anything to write home about. It was probably quite exciting, and I'm sure catching glimpses of the fox as she gave us a merry chase across the manicured pastures and through the sylvan glens was thrilling for those who were paying attention. But I was doing everything I could just to stay horsed and not make a fool of myself among all these avid equestrians. This wasn't anything like riding the range in the West.

Luckily, no one noticed what a novice I was. And in

the hour of cooling down from the blooded excitement of siccing a pack of frenzied hounds on a tiny red fox, when we were all standing around and stroking the flanks of fine horse flesh on the lawn of Five Oaks, each sipping his or her preferred form of southern comfort, I was amused to see that I had become a center of attention. Several of the women—and men—had taken a fancy to me and were floating around me, trying to solve the mystery of Bob and Bill's houseguest.

I had gleaned during the hunt that my hosts were, indeed, twins named Bob and Bill and were fabulously wealthy and extremely powerful in whatever they did and, other than joining in the hunt, were reclusive and seldom in residence at Five Oaks.

While I was spinning lies about my devised-on-the-fly Kentucky roots and charming the pants and panties off my admirers—or at least so it seemed they wished, as evidenced by the young beauty with the thick southern drawl who tucked a card with her telephone number in my waistband—one of the twins stood off to the aside and assessed my every move through slitted eyes. The other twin had disappeared as soon as the first riders to depart started loading their horse trailers.

Eventually, the crowd had thinned down considerably beyond a hopeful handful clinging to my elbow. At this point, the twin must have had enough, because he rudely cut through the ring around me and took me by the arm and said he wanted to show me something in the barn.

I could hear the something he wanted to show me as we approached the barn, which was set off a good hundred yards from the house.

When we entered the structure and my eyes adjusted to the dimness and the straw chaff floating in the air, I saw that the missing twin had a naked Eric bent over a bale of hay, topped by a horse blanket, and was riding him hard from the rear.

Eric was doing a good deal of grunting and groaning and praising of the twin's performance, but I sort of had the idea that he was doing it to please and because it was expected of him. The glistening of the light sweat on Eric's undulating

103

muscles under the onslaught of "no slouch himself" twin was a real turn on. The twin was holding Eric's cheek down on the horse blanket roughly with a hand spread out on his bald head, and Eric watched me as I entered the barn.

"See you started without me, Bob," the twin who had brought me into the barn said. That cleared up for me who was who.

Then Bill turned to me. "Strip off the jacket and shirt. Leave the jodhpurs and boots on."

I stripped slowly, exhibition style, but, in my mind, I was doing so for Eric, not for the clients. Eric rewarded me by widening his eyes and smiling big as I pulled my shirt off and slitting his eyes in an obvious reverie of lust. He grunted and twitched as Bob pulled back almost full length and jammed his cock back inside the chocolate muscle man's ass with great force.

While I was slowly shedding down to the jodhpurs, Bill had more quickly stripped down and had moved deeper into the dimly lit barn.

"Come over here. Now." There was no question that Bill was to be obeyed.

I moved back into the barn, and my eyes opened wide in surprise. Bill was astride some sort of padded pommel horse contraption supported by a grounded center pole, like they used in gymnastics, although it looked more like what they had in some of those pseudo-Western bars with the mechanical horse rides. It had a saddle strapped to the top, stirrups and all. Bill was in the saddle, completely nude. He was angled up at the back of the saddle and was pulling on his meat. His cock was long, if a bit thinnish. And it already was very hard.

"Climb up, facing away from me," he commanded.

I put a foot in a stirrup and swung my other leg up in front of me as gracefully as I could and over the contraption. Bill held me by the hips as I swung over, helping me to hold steady. I came down wedged in front of him in the saddle, with his long, hard cock throbbing up the small of my back. When I was saddled, Bill reached down at both sides and activated straps across my ankles in the stirrups so that I now was trapped there.

Then he began to make love to me as my butt was firmly wedged against his pelvis. Big beefy, hairy arms encircled me, and he was kissing the back of my neck and running his hands all over my torso, palming at last one hand over one of my nipples and digging below my waistband and inside the supporter cup with the other hand to cover my cock and balls and bring me to the game down there. He was moving his pelvis up and down, dry fucking the small of my back with his dick. He was the client and this was kind of nice anyway, so I moaned for him and moved my body against his. And I turned my lips to his and we kissed deeply.

"Raise up in the stirrups," he commanded in a hoarse voice, and I did as he directed.

I felt the back seam of the tight jodhpurs split as his fingers tugged at the edges, and I no longer had to wonder if the seams of the breeches would hold. He drew a tube of lube out of a side pocket on the pommel horse contraption and palmed my belly with one hand while the lubed fingers of the other hand slid through the slitted seam and worked inside my ass. I heard a condom packet being ripped open and saw it land on the floor of the barn shortly before he was tipping me forward and then pulling me back onto his long, throbbing tool.

As he slid into me, I groaned and grunted for him and gave a little cry of invasion and arched my back and threw my arms and head back, pulling his lips to mine in an "Oh fuck me!" maneuver that I knew worked so well with the clients at this point.

We writhed together for several minutes, with me declaring how good he was, how filling he was, how I'd never had it this good.

And then the surprise was on me. The pommel horse was shuddering and the other twin was now swinging up into the saddle as well. Facing me. Grabbing me by the hips, as Bill palmed my pecs and leaned back, tipping our hips up. Forcing the head of his cock at the entrance of my channel, already stuffed with Bill's cock. Pushing a lever somewhere that caused the stirrups to rise and spread, opening my legs further. Giving Bob's cock room to force itself inside me, alongside Bill's. No more acting at this point. I was double stuffed and stretched to the limit. I cried out and groaned and grunted.

And Bill holding his cock steady and hard and deep inside me, Bob began moving his cock in and out, rubbing against my walls, caressing his brother's cock, moving deeper, ever deeper. I was panting and trying to catch my breath. Hands roaming all over me and over each other, lips kissing me and each other. A cacophony of moaning and groaning and sighing.

I glanced wildly to the side as I sensed movement inside the barn at the periphery of my vision. A chocolate mass of fluid muscle coming into view. Eric approaching closer. Watching the fucking in the saddle on the pommel horse. A magnificently compact body of glistening muscle. Eric was stroking his own, huge, thick cock as he watched the twins double me. He was licking his lips. I had a brief vision of being tripled and almost fainted from the shock of how sensually, if physically impossible, I felt about that.

Another switch was thrown and the pommel horse began to gently rock back and forward on the center pole. A heightening of sensation, an effect on the cocks inside me that went beyond the control of the twins.

Was it me or was the rolling increasing in intensity, becoming bucking? No, it was. Oh Gaaawd. The twins crying out in passion. Me joining them in chorus. Bucking, bucking, bucking. The cocks fucking, fucking, fucking, sent churning by the bucking horse. Oh, Gawwd, oh Gawwd. Losing it. Shooooting Offfff.

Not ending there, however; the mechanical contraption continuing to buck and roll until long after the twins had played my channel like a counterpunching piston engine and made their deposits and finished with their shouts of climaxing lust in two-part harmony.

Off the horse now, unentangled. Bob just grabbed up his clothes and strode out of the barn. Bill motioned to Eric and, between them, they moved me over to the bale of hay with the horse blanket on it and laid me gently down on my back.

"Clean up here and then bring the car around at six," Bill said to Eric in that "to be obeyed" tone both the twins had. "We're going into Middleburg for dinner." And then he was gone as well.

Eric dipped a cloth in a nearby trough of water and came over and started dabbing my face and torso with the cool cloth. I put my hand on the back of his hand and let it slide up his forearm and across his bulging bicep, pulling his face down to mine, taking his lips in mine. I spread my legs and wrapped them around his beefy thighs and pulled him into me. Big hands, big feet, bald head, all panned out in this package. The power of him was swinging like a baseball bat between his legs.

I threw my head back and arched my back and cried out for him as he entered me with the thick, thick dick of his, and I bucked hard against him, riding hard, enjoying him as he was enjoying me in waves and waves of freely offered fucking.

* * * *

I was toweling myself off after a long, languid bath in the well-appointed bathroom off the scarlet room that evening when I heard the soft knock on the door.

When I opened the door, Eric entered with a supper tray for me. I'd been told I had to stay in the room for the remainder of my stay. I moved to embrace him, but he leaned away from me, put a thick finger up to his lips and then pointed to the corners of the ceiling. I looked up and saw the small flickering of pinpoint lights. Of course. What happened in this room was being video recorded.

I let him go with regret, ate the dinner and put the tray outside the door, and then I unwrapped the towel from my waist, threw it into the bathroom, and went back to the canopy bed. Stretching myself out on the bed on my back, I masturbated and writhed sensuously on the bed for the benefit of the camera for a short while and then I went into a semiconscious doze. It had been an exhausting assignment. I

107

couldn't remember whether I had ever been as inventively and fully fucked.

When I woke, the room was dark except for the flickering light from the fire in the fireplace. One of the twins was at the fireplace, perhaps having just lit it. He was naked, facing the fire. His legs were spread, and I could see his long cock dangling between his legs, picking up the light coming off the fire. He turned at hearing me stir, and I began to learn that the twins were not identical in their preferences.

He, who I later guessed was Bill, motioned me over to the fireplace.

"Kneel on the oriental carpet here and suck me," He commanded. His voice wasn't as hard edged as it had been earlier that day.

While I sucked on his dick, bringing it to life, and fingered his balls, he poured himself a glass of wine and held the glass in one hand and cupped the back of my head with his other hand. I was pleasing him. I certainly knew how to do that well.

When he was fully engorged, he pulled my head back off his cock with his fingers in my hair. I twitched with surprise as I saw the wine bottle in his hand as I arched back. He tipped it, letting wine spill down over my chest. Then he put the bottle down, came down on his knees in front of me. Wrapping one strong, beefy arm around the small of my back as I was arched back on my knees, my head reaching back almost to the floor, he started to lick the wine down my torso, until his lips reached and swallowed my cock. I just lay back supported by his forearm around the small of my back, my arms hanging at my side and staring into the flickering fire in the fireplace as he sucked me to ejaculation.

Then he turned me onto my knees, my chest flat on the carpet, my eyes still glued to the firelight, as he opened a condom packet and crowned himself. The packet fluttered to the carpet beside my face, and then he crouched over my hips and took me doggy style in long, smooth, slow strokes.

While he was fucking me, I heard someone enter the room. Eric, perhaps? And when Bill had ejaculated and pushed me down on the carpet and moved sensuously on my body with his as he kissed my neck and shoulders and we both watched the fire until we had calmed down, he escorted me to the bathroom, where a warm bath had been drawn. We went into the tub, facing each other, and then we both drank wine, while I let my toes bring his cock back to life. With a little cry of passion, he grabbed my butt cheeks and pulled my hips into his pelvis. I let my legs rise out of the tub and planted the soles of my feet on the tiles on either side of his head. He held my hips with his strong hands and I used the leverage of my feet on the walls to fuck myself on his regenerated tool.

One satisfied client.

The other twin, Bob, I'm sure, was a whole other story. He silently entered the room late that night. I was barely awake as he bound my wrists over my head at the headboard. I was quite awake, though, as he was trussing up my legs in the apparatus at the foot of the bed that spread my legs wide and lifted both them and my pelvis.

He roughly gagged me with the rubber ball gag I'd seen in the nightstand drawer earlier. Then he lubed up and used a progression of ever larger, ever more knobbly dildos on my ass channel while I writhed on the bed and tried to scream around the rubber ball filling my mouth and pushing my tongue down.

That little excitement over, he jerked the gag off. He wanted to hear me when he was taking me himself. I watched him take a strap-on cock enlarger out of the drawer. It had suction cup-like knobs running around it in a screw pattern. I watched as he lubed himself, rolled on a condom, and then strapped on the apparatus. I begged him not to do this, just as I knew he wanted me to do. I trembled for him and stammered my fear. And I knew this excited him. He walked over to where I had left my riding clothes and took up the riding crop I'd dropped there.

He was flicking it as he approached me between my spread and raised legs, and I whimpered for him. I cried out as he wanted me to and arched my back up and down on the bed and struggled as best I could as he screwed his enhanced tool inside me. I grunted and groaned for him as he started stroking inside me and flicking my butt cheeks and flanks with the riding crop.

After a while, he pulled out of me, freed his long, hard cock from the enhancer, pulled off the condom, and climbed up on the bed and straddled my chest. He fed his cock into my mouth and I sucked him expertly, as I knew he expected me to. He pulled out of me and shot all over my chest with a throaty cry.

Then he moved to a nearby short-back boudoir chair and just sat there, watching me, naked and all trussed up, and fingering and pulling on his cock.

I could see that he was beginning to breath heavily and getting big again, and I wondered what he had planned for round two.

But, inexplicably, he stood and started releasing me from the bonds.

"You can go clean yourself up now," he said in a low, hoarse voice when I was free.

I stumbled off the bed, sore and exhausted from my full day of making money the old fashioned way, and started to hobble toward the bathroom.

But that was the signal for round two. Bob grabbed me by the hair from the back and propelled me to and astride the chair he'd been sitting in with a fist in the small of my back. The breath went out of me as I fell across the chair. He was at me like a thundering animal in full rut. Yanking my head back with a fist in my hair and thrusting hard between my butt cheeks with his long, hard cock. Fucking me and fucking me and fucking me.

I gave him what he wanted. Complete subservience and cries of being cruelly split asunder—which wasn't all that much off the mark.

Another satisfied client.

* * * *

The next morning Eric drove me back to the airport in the Lincoln limo. I missed the scheduled flight and had to rebook for later, because Eric stopped the car near the end of the drive and joined me in the back seat, where, first, he pushed my head down between his legs for me to suck him as he sat back in the seat and spread them, and then lifted me and sat my channel down on his thick tool while I rocked back and forth on top of him to our eventual mutual satisfaction.

It was only when the plane was half way back across the continent that I realized why Leon had really been grinning. The twins had first fucked me through a slit in the jodhpurs and had at no point commented on the platinum hair, shaved chest and pits, or the V of the bush. They didn't give a flying fuck about this. Leon had told me to do that just as his own private joke. Well, fuck him—but not in this lifetime, I hoped.

Chapter 11: Governored

The limo was where I expected it to be in the VIP parking lot of the airport serving the capital city of the forgettable southern state located between somewhere and somewhere else. For those of us from the West Coast, most of these states down in this region are forgettable.

The Limo wasn't parked up at the well-lit side near the terminal but back toward the end of the lot and close up to some bushes on the side away from the terminal. No one was near the vehicle, but the doors were unlocked. After looking around to be pretty sure I wasn't seen, I quietly opened a rear door that was almost pushed into the bushes and slipped into the backseat. There was a pile of luggage on the floor near the center, and I crawled over that and pulled a blanket over my head. This would have all been easier to accomplish—and not so warm and stuffy—if I hadn't been wearing a three-piece suit. These were the instructions, though. Blend in. Do what you have to do and not be caught at it.

Some minutes later I heard the driver's door open and we were off. So far so good.

After an eternity of bone-rattling rapid speed, probably on an expressway from the sound of vehicles passing and being passed, and then slowing down to the stop-and-go movement of an urban area, the limo stopped. The driver exited the vehicle. Several long minutes of silence. Then I heard the rear door on the other side of the limo from where I was hidden open and the vehicle settle as at least one person got in the backseat. There was considerable noise coming from beyond the confines of the limo while the door was open. The sound of a crowd. Boisterous conversation and laughter. It sounded happy. I burrowed farther under the blanket. This was no time to be seen.

"Fuckin' opera," a deep, gruff voice said as the door slammed shut and the sound of the crowd deadened. "Some year we're gonna have enough in the coffers sos I don't have to attend these fuckin' operas and perform for the Devonshire set. Right, Steve?"

"Yes sir, right." Another, softer, a little higher-pitched, more refined voice.

I heard the driver's door open, more crowd noise, the seat I was wedged against puff back a bit, a breeze of air, and then the door shut and, with a honk, we were pulling away from a curb again.

"You bring the latest budget proposal folder?" The commanding voice.

"Yes, sir, right here, sir." The subservient voice.

"And the plans for the new nuclear plant they want to put downstate. I promised I'd look at those before Monday too. Fuckin' power company. They said they were lookin' at another state when they endorsed me. Now I'm stuck with their fuckin' fallout."

"Right, sir. They're right here. The plans, I have them here in my briefcase."

"Because you know we have to go straight to the airport from here. God, I hate these unexpected trips to Washington. I'd planned to have some foolin' around time this weekend. Did cha cancel the hotel rooms at the Omni?"

"Yes, Sir. And made reservations at the Mayflower in D.C., just as you asked. Two adjoining rooms."

I groaned to myself. This was supposed to be all over right here in this town. Well, I'd just have to adjust.

"Fuckin' opera."

A foot had come around the stack of suitcases and was nudging me in the thigh. "OK, son, you can come up now."

He was still talking as I came up from under the blanket and turned, and with "the dominant voice" pulling me and turning me, I plopped down on the limo backseat between two suits, one on a bulky middle-aged man of noticeable height, and one on a younger, Harvard Law School grad type. Tanned. Well groomed. Quite good-looking.

There was no question who was in charge. The larger guy was already pawing at me. Prodding and feeling, like I was the Pillsbury Dough Boy.

"Well, lookie what we have here. A real stud. Does his picture justice. Yes Siree, a real hunk."

It was pretty dark in the car; we were already moving out of the well-lit city center and onto an expressway. Back to the airport, if I'd heard right.

But I knew who he was. "Client 11" was all that Leon had said when he gave me the assignment back in L.A. But he'd said it in the hushed tones he reserved for the regular big spenders whose files were kept separate, more private than the others.

I'd seen him on TV. He'd had his hat in the ring for the presidency in early primaries last year but had been weeded out as too folksy, too reactionary conservative, and from a state no one could remember and didn't particularly care about. He was the governor of that state, though, so he wasn't necessarily a nobody. And if he could afford what he was paying for me, he most certainly wasn't a nobody.

"Excuse me? What was that?" I'd heard him say something, give some sort of command, but I'd been dreaming, catching up on the situation. I liked to try to keep up.

"I said whip it out, son. Let's see your dick. Umm, yes, very nice. A good buy. Now suck on this."

My face was in his lap for most of the rest of the trip to the airport. His cock had seemed sort of shriveled—but quite thick—when I first closed my lips over it, but it wasn't any time at all before it was a real gagger. And he was all business;

not only was he able to maintain a running conversation with his hunky "go for" assistant on schedules and the state of legislative bills, but he was also able to get his hips moving, and he jacked off in pretty quick order. When I felt him about ready to come, I moved to pull my mouth off him, but he just took my head in his strong, beefy hands and held me down in his tool until he'd spouted and I'd swallowed it all and cleaned his cock for him with my tongue. Winner take all style. Sucking—and, certainly ingesting—wasn't my favorite sex act. But when the client pays what the client pays for my services, the client gets what the client wants.

After ejaculating, the governor took time out from his busy schedule to stroke on my cock and to hold my head back against the seat with a fist in my hair and do some lip exploration of my neck and cheeks and mouth—and tongue and tonsils.

As we were pulling into the airport, he left off and rapid-fired instructions at me.

"Back under the blanket, stud. After leaving Steve and me off at the jet ramp, the limo will pull around to the baggage stairs. You can go up there while helping the driver to load up the luggage into the plane. Anyone try to take your photograph, turn your head—or your ass is grass. There's a seat back in that compartment where you can sit for takeoff. When I let you know it's time to come into the passenger compartment, be stripped down to your socks."

And, of course it went as the governor instructed. The limo driver wouldn't make eye contact with me while we were loading the plane, and he would jerk back whenever our hands made contact in moving the suitcases. It was like he wanted to be able to deny I ever was there, like he was already contemplating his congressional testimony. A good move on his part, actually, I thought. It didn't bother me much. I'd often gotten that from the hired help. On the other hand, I often liked the hired help better than the client, and I often wound up giving it to them for free. Sometimes I even did it in the spirit of rubbing it in the client's face—without him or her knowing it, of course—that they had to pay big bucks and their cook or bodyguard got it for free. If they were arousing enough.

The driver was old and bald and pretty dumpy, though, so no regrets that I was invisible to him. Now Steve, the Harvard grad flunky, on the other hand . . .

When I was summoned after we were airborne and presumably flying northeast, I was ready. And upon entering the passenger compartment from the baggage area, I did a pose in the doorway. The usual pose for the client early on to give them a thrill. The governor only grunted and raised his bushy eyebrows a bit, but I could see that he was impressed and happy because the front of his briefs tented right up. That's all he was wearing now, his briefs. And in his current state of near nakedness, he gave a first impression of being a big Russian bear. The man towered to well over six and a half feet and he had the bulk to match that. It probably helped him a lot in dominating his political opponents. It wouldn't take a genius to know what his likely sexual preferences were. He was a little on the hefty side, just slightly paunchy, but also heavily muscled. And black curly hair all over him.

"Nice bod," he said. "And damn well it should be. You can tell your pimping managers that the last price hike has almost ejected their sticky fingers from my pocketbook. So, you can start earning your pay right now. See that conference table up front?"

I did. Not a very wide table because of the narrow fuselage of this private Jetstream, but maybe four feet wide and seven feet long, running down the center aisle from which regular airplane seats had been taken out. There were a couple of pull-up chairs with upholstery matching the plane seats on either side of the table. The governor was up there pulling them to the sides.

Steve, meanwhile, was sitting closer to me, in a section of facing seats on my right. Still fully dressed in a smart, dark business suit, he was making like he was deeply involved in a stack of papers on his lap, and he had a laptop open on the pull-down tray of the seat next to him, by the window. But I could see that he was copping shots at me. He was blushing. I couldn't gauge whether he was interested or embarrassed by it all— but

117

having seen it all several times before. I was quite sure of that. All part of the job.

Well, this is all part of *my* job, too, buddy, was what I was thinking. But I was also thinking he looked interesting. A redhead, more auburn than carrot, though, and very well put together—at least in a business suit. Slim hips, wide shoulders, good depth to his chest. Maybe we'd just have to see about Steve. This governor was one client I wouldn't mind doing an upside-down social payment screwing job on. Much too self-centered and pleased with himself. He wasn't even from my party.

"We're gonna use this table for a massage," the governor was saying. "There are towels and oil over here. Set the table up, and then I want a massage. It's been a rough day topped by a fuckin' opera fund-raiser. I want everything sucked after my muscles are unstressed. Fingers, toes, dick, the whole enchilada. Chop, chop. Earn your pay."

I pride myself on my full body massage, and I had the governor as loose and as close to cooing as he would ever get short of an electoral college win. He particularly liked the finger and toe sucking. He'd had the cock sucking before, but I was more inventive this time, and he had to grab my head by the hair and pull me off of him to keep from shooting off. This told me his intention was that I was going to be topped and probably sooner than later.

A little later, it turned out, because he wanted to be fucked. I turned him on his stomach and licked into the cavernous gorge between his mountainous, hairy buns and tongued him around the rim and into the hole until he was writhing under me. Then, at his command, I started to go up on the table and then remembered and looked around in the nearby plane seats.

"Ummm. Where? Where are the . . .?"

"For what I'm paying, we don' need no rubbers," the governor muttered. "They guarantee clean and I expect skin. Get up here. Fuck me."

And so I did. I climbed up on the table and straddled his hips and ran my engorging cock up and down inside his crack, and across his hole, again and again, while he started melting and begging for it and I was getting hard enough to give him a proper fuck.

On the last downward pull of the cock, I pressed it down as I started up again, and the dickhead just plopped into the hole and I glided inside. He was loose and warm inside. He brought his rear up to my pelvis a bit off the table as dogs do when they present themselves, and I had him grunting and groaning nicely in a long stroke session of deep slides and some rotating work.

Not being sure what he wanted me to do when I shot off, I pulled out of him and ejaculated up the small of his back into a thatch of dark, curly hair. He didn't object, so I must have guessed right.

Right after that, though, he bounded right off the table and grabbed me and practically threw me into one of the facing seats across the aisle from where Steve was sitting, studiously pretending he wasn't seeing or hearing anything.

"Scoot your butt down. Legs over chair arms. Now."

He was pouring oil on his engorged, thick cock while he was saying this, and I thought I'd get at least some of the oil in my channel before he fucked me. But I was wrong.

He was crouched between my legs. The briefs had come off a long time ago. And he was squeezing and lifting my butt cheeks off of the chair seat, pulling me up toward his pelvis. When he had the bulb of his dickhead rubbing at my entrance, he just reared his hips back and thrust himself inside me and pumped me like an animal in full rut.

He had marvelous staying power and vigor for a man his age. And a thicker cock than most of my clients, the strength and working of his cock inside me all the more focusing because I hadn't been opened up well before he was porking me and because I didn't often get the sensation of skin sliding back and forth inside me between my ass walls and his steely shaft. He wasn't cut. I enjoyed being fucked by uncut cocks, the extra sliding sensation of it. And as brutal and direct as the governor's fucking was, I quite enjoyed it.

I wondered idly if Steve was enjoying it too. Not just

being a limited voyeur to what the governor was doing to me, since I saw no evidence that Steve was watching with any sort of attention or stroking himself while we were doing it, but also turned on by the assault. I also sort of wondered if the governor fucked Steve too.

There was no wondering what he was going to do when he finally, after a good half hour of vigorous pumping, shot his load in one explosive victory celebration. He had brought his cock out to the rim of my hole for the event, ejaculated into my entrance, and then returned to pumping me for several more minutes. This wind-down session was actually the most pleasurable for me, because there was extra lubricant inside me now.

I was summarily banished to the baggage compartment for the descent into Washington, D.C.'s, Ronald Reagan airport, just across the Potomac from the federal city.

We had two adjoining rooms at the Mayflower Hotel, across town from the airport. I was booked in Steve's room under a name I barely had a chance to see on the register sheet in passing. The governor, of course, was alone in his room.

But, not really alone for long. Once we were settled and I'd taken a shower in Steve's bathroom, the governor made clear I was going to be in his bed—and that he was going to get as much of his money's worth out of me as he could. When I entered the room, I couldn't see him. He came in behind me, twisted my arms behind my back, and propelled me toward the bed. He bent me over forward when we got there and pushed my chest down on the bedspread. He immediately started probing my canal with the fingers of his other hand, which, thankfully, were lubricated. They were digging deep inside me, and I was moving my hips for him and moaning and groaning, just as I knew rough dominators liked. I was groaning for real, though, as he started working his cock in between the fingers without extracting them. And then he was plowing and riding me hard. That loose foreskin of his cock moving back and forth between the rock hardness of his tool and my sensitive ass walls.

An amazing man. Who could have thought that he

could jack off four times that night while he rode me hard and into the wee hours of the morning? But I was used to this; clients usually did do everything they could to stretch out every dollar they were paying for my services.

At dawn he threw me out of his room, and I took another shower in Steve's bathroom and curled up on a loveseat by the television set. Steve was sleeping blissfully on one of the double beds in the room, snoring slightly. He was sleeping in the nude and had thrown the sheets off. The cut of him in his suit didn't lie. He was in very nice shape and had a very presentable cock and two nice, pouty balls. If my ass hadn't been worn out by the governor, I would have put a move on Steve. But maybe I'd get a chance later.

Later came sooner. I felt a cramp from all the work underneath the governor and uncoiled myself from an uncomfortable position on the love seat and walked over to the open door between the two rooms. I had been thinking of what the governor had said the last time he was fucking me from behind on the bed, me on my knees and presenting to him with raised butt, his slight bulge of a paunch rubbing up and down the small of my back, his hairy chest slapping against my shoulder blades, and me hanging onto the headboard for dear life while he dug fingernails into my nipples and took me in long thrusts. He'd said he liked me so much we'd do some special fucking the next night. I wondered what that meant, and I didn't like surprises. So, I'd been drawn to the door with half a notion of going through his luggage to see what kind of toys he might have. He'd do what he wanted, of course, but I liked to be prepared for the most taxing to come. I stood in the doorway, leaning against the frame, and taking in the room. Where to start looking first?

"He won't be back until after noon."

I turned. The Harvard grad was awake. He was sitting up, knees drawn to chin, watching me. He hadn't covered himself, and he was looking mighty fine. All reddish sheen and sculpted muscle. A half smile, promising more if I worked it right. A lock of curly hair tumbling down toward one hazel-green eye.

"He had some meeting this morning. He wouldn't tell me what it was. Rather strange. He doesn't keep much secret from me . . . naturally." The smile was broader now, a little wry. A very nice smile. "That's why we had to come to Washington unexpectedly today. But he did tell me that the meeting would take all morning. Said he wouldn't need me until after lunch."

Ah, a great opening then. "Than what could we possibly do while we wait?" I asked, giving him my best sheepish smile.

A slight pause.

"We could order room service for starters."

"Why, isn't there enough service available in the room already?" I moved into my best "I'm available" lounging pose against the frame of the door and opened my smile up more for him.

His tone turned to regret. "Nice idea, but way out of my league. I make the governor's arrangements. I know what you cost. There's no way I could afford you."

"You haven't asked what I'd charge," I responded quietly. Giving him my "I'm serious" look.

"Uhh?"

"Two condoms. Two used condoms—used by you, with me. For you, that's all I'd charge."

He moved gracefully to me, although I could see he was trembling with surprise and anticipation. And he moaned deeply as I knelt before him in the doorway and made love to his very nice cock.

He was on his back on the bed, me astride his hips and rising and falling on his throbbing tool, him gurgling softly, undulating languidly, and holding my hips in his hands, for the first half of the payment. We took our time in the second half, making love properly, using all of our bodies and all of our tactile sensations. He lay full length behind me, both of us on our sides, and he explored my body with one hand, as I turned my head to him in a long, lingering, exploring kiss and raised my leg to give his cock deeper access to my channel. I gave him the full treatment, wanting it as much as he did after a night of mostly being just a hole for the governor to work to his private, singular power trip.

The irony. The governor paying big bucks so that his harried assistant could get the better-quality fuck.

I was so pleased that I demanded a third used condom as my tip. I'd sent him to the showers and then surprised him by joining him there, turning him toward and facing me, my back against the slick tiled wall. Then I hiked my legs up on his hips and took his lips in mine, and groaned and moaned from him as he moved my back up and down on the tiles under the flowing water from the showerhead with the thrusts of his cock inside me.

After we were done, he told me profusely how much he'd enjoyed it, but then he said, "But I don't understand why—why me, and why for free?"

"You're a hunk, I've got to tell you, if no one else has. And don't you get tired of working for 'the man'? Aren't there times you'd like to tell him to go screw himself."

"Yeah, sometimes," he answered in a low voice.

"Well, this is both of us telling him he can just go screw himself."

* * * *

He was dressing and I was drying off with a towel when we both heard the heavy knock at the door to the governor's room. The "do not disturb" signs were out, so it shouldn't be maid service.

Steve turned to me, put a finger to his lips, and motioned for me to get out of view of the connecting doors. I gathered up parts of my suit and my socks and shoes and moved over to the door to the corridor and hurriedly dressed as Steve turned and went to the other door.

I didn't hear it all, but I did hear the part about "IRS agents" and "Checking irregularities" and "The governor down at our office" and "We understand you keep his accounts, Mr. Horton," and "Please finish getting dressed and come with us."

I didn't want to hear any more, though, and knew I was

123

just the spanner in the works that neither Steve nor the governor needed around here at the moment. I quietly opened the door to the corridor; checked to see if the coast was clear, which it was; and closed the door again as silently as I could before moving as quickly and quietly as I could away from the door to the governor's room and toward the bank of the Mayflower elevators.

I wasn't worried about myself; I always came prepared for the eventuality of needing a quick getaway and had plenty of resources to get back to L.A. And I certainly didn't give too figs for whatever trouble the governor had landed in. I was worried a bit about Steve, though. Steve had been very nice.

And I worried about the ire of Leon, my pimp. I sure hoped the services to the governor had been prepaid—and in untraceable money.

Chapter 12: Prepped

Not for the first time I didn't like the gleam in Leon's eye or the lilt in his voice when he handed me my assignment. He was much too pleased with himself when he hand me the envelope containing the address and the gate key. We'd been getting along better than usual lately—or had been up to the time he seemed to think that meant I was warming to him and he propositioned me again and I turned him down flat again. But if there was a little twist to this assignation, at least it would be short-lived. The address was right here in the city. The Gordan Institute up in the Hollywood Hills.

I knew this to be a tony private plastic surgery hospital for those who wanted to be recarved without losing sight of their swimming pools and movie star mansions. Not because I'd done anything like that myself, of course. I was still at my peak, thank you, very much, and wouldn't need any of that sort of help for a good ten years more. Depending, though, I guessed, on what I did between now and then to earn my pay. And when I did need plastic surgery, there was no way I was going to be able to afford the Gordan Institute.

I just hoped that Leon hadn't agreed to let me get sliced up.

"So, what costume?" I asked.

"Oh, just go as you are," Leon answered. And then he laughed. "Chances are you won't be wearing it long anyway."

I took the envelope from Leon's claws and gave him a wan "you don't intimidate me—much" smile and headed my Beamer convertible up slope. It was late afternoon on a Sunday and it was "another damn beautiful" day enhanced by the relative lack of bumper-to-bumper traffic.

I halfway knew where the Gordan Institute was, and I found it without too much trouble, hulking behind a high stuccoed privacy wall next door to what had once been Bela Lugosi's haunted manse. Leon had given me a plastic key card like they use for hotel room entry, and it opened up the iron gates at the institute a charm. No one was about as I drove in and parked next to a silver Mercedes convertible in an otherwise empty, bricked-over parking pad. By the time I got to the front entrance, hidden in the shadows behind a porte cochere, no doubt designed for privacy in arrival and departure of the well-heeled patients, the entry door was opening, and I could see there was at least one other person besides me here on a Sunday. The absence of other cars disturbed me a bit. This was a residential facility; was there some sort of law against rich people getting tummy tucks on weekends in May, I wondered.

"You were sent by the agency?" a well-modulated baritone voice asked from the depths beyond the opening door.

"Umm, yes. Alphonse?"

"Come in. Yes, yes, you'll do nicely."

I knew that. He didn't have to tell me that. They charged three thou an hour for my attentions. And for that I did quite a bit more than "nicely."

The door swung open, and I was facing "Alphonse." He wasn't really Alphonse. I knew that, and I'm sure he knew I knew that. His mug, no matter how many times it had been redone, was well known in town. He was Grant Gordan, the celebrated magic surgeon of beauty. This was his institute.

He was playing doctor. Starched, stark-white three-quarter-length doctor's smock over soft-cotton, institutional green scrubs that somehow still gave the impression they had been tailored and cost a bundle. Crinkling transparent plastic booties on what looked like gray bedroom slippers. He was tricked out to be playing the senior physician in a long-running television medical drama. Gray-haired, in his fifties, but handsome, and chiseled to an epitome of perfection that only a millionaire's billfold or an "in the business" discount could provide. A very nice bedside smile that, alone, would have cost me a fortune.

"Oh, excuse me," I stammered. "Did I get the day or time wrong? Have I interrupted a procedure?"

"No, no, of course not. You're right on time. No procedures today. We're undergoing renovations this week, so no procedures at all. No patients in residence."

"Oh, but—"

"Oh, these. I was just trying on a new shipment of surgical wear. Dr. Gordan just had these sent in."

Hokay, I thought. It's your ten thou, "Alphonse," I thought. I had peeked at Leon's chart—as I always tried to do so I knew when I should be going off the clock. This guy had bought four hours and gotten a discount of two thousand for booking that block of time. This almost always meant at least a double, but I was just as happy if they thought of that in advance and padded the time. Often trying to hammer a recharge and second fucking into an hour—or even two hours—became quite frustrating for the client and often played out in their attitude as something unpleasant.

"Follow me, please." And with that, "Alphonse" turned and walked briskly down a corridor leading off to the right of the plush reception room that, with its big stone fireplace, vaulted ceiling, and big expanse of glass overlooking a sea of green grass and majestic pines, looked more like the living room in a mountain lodge than a hospital waiting room.

I followed in the wake of the crinkling noise his surgical booties were making with the thought that, if I had known we were going to play doctor, I would have seen if Leon had a nurse's uniform in his wardrobe room.

I was ushered into a large, wood-paneled room with

book-lined walls except for one well-lit panel that sported what I'm sure was meant to be an impressive number of framed university diplomas, medical licenses, honorary plaques, and photos of "Alphonse" shaking hands with various extremely well-preserved movie stars and industry titans of old—or at least of older age than they had been made to appear.

The mahogany desk was massive, the throne behind it that "Alphonse" perched in momentarily was massive, and the sort of wheel chair contraption he waved my butt into was nothing short of strange. It was a comfortable chair and all that, but did he put his prospective clients into wheel chairs this early in the sales pitch? I didn't have time to let this thought percolate, however.

"I trust you've been told the scenario and the service."

"Ummm. No, actually," I said.

"Oh, well, then," Alphonse said. "I do have a contract, you know. And the money's been paid."

"Good, fine," I said. I couldn't think of anything else to say. I was busy racking Leon over in my brain. I knew there was a reason for that evil little smile. Holding the particulars back from me again. Such a poor loser.

By then Alphonse had bounded back out of his—or, rather, Dr. Gordan's—throne and was nervously flitting around the room.

"Strip down, please. I want to see if my directions were followed."

I stood up from the wheel chair and started to take off my clothes, in the slow, provocative way I'd been taught to do, wondering all the time whether I was supposed to wear something I hadn't been told about. As I did so, Alphonse came around to the edge of the desk facing me and perched there, closely scrutinizing my every movement. I imagined that I was a client asking for a little more here and a little less there, and I wondered if he also was thinking about how I could be recarved to best advantage.

But his eyes were slitted, and he was humming softly to himself. From long experience, I recognized this as a sign of satisfaction with the goods.

"Ah, yes," he said when I was stripped down, giving out a sigh and letting his hand run across his crotch. "Nice body hair. And a natural blond, I see."

Well, no, but he didn't need to know all that was entailed in that.

"Sit, please."

I did so, and Alphonse was back on the move. He was behind me, and I heard the noise of something being dragged toward me. I looked around in time to see some sort of steel contraption on wheels, supporting a large cylinder, rolling up to my chair. But that's all the time I had to see anything, as the doctor was right behind me then, throwing his arms around my chest, holding me down into the wheel chair with one arm and clamping a mask over my mouth and nose with the other. I struggled briefly, but not for long. The gas was fast and effective.

When I came to, I was strapped down on my back on a white-paper-covered steel operating table. My wrists were bound close behind my head, which pulled my arms up and close beside my head on either side. My ankles were bound too, but to flexible appendages that extended beyond the end of the table, which only reached to the small of my back. It was apparent that these appendages could be manipulated apart and up and even folded to bend my legs.

I awoke to a whimper. It was mine.

"Ah, good, awake. Be aware that I contracted for the specific service."

I focused on the voice. Alphonse—Grant Gordan—all smiles and standing over me with an aerosol can in one hand and in the other—a straight razor.

"Oh, God, no," I muttered. "Please—"

"You must hold very still, or this will undoubtedly hurt you more than it does me," Gordan murmured. And then he smiled. I knew the look in those eyes. He was aroused.

He started squirting foam onto my torso and into my pits. It was cold, and I squirmed a bit. I said nothing; I was still assessing the situation and how and whether to get out of it. Just how crazy was he? Was this just the first stage of something pretty horrific? He lifted the razor and I stopped squirming. I wasn't that stupid.

He had music going on in the background. Just what I was used to hearing when I went into a dentist's office. And he was humming as he worked.

The razor moved from my right pit to my left pit. This was followed by Gordan's tongue, as he lapped up the residual lather there, which must have been something other than soap, because he was having a good slurping time of it.

"You know," he said as he finished there and was carefully shaving around my nipples and along my hairline down to my navel, "For years I watched my patients being prepped by the nurses before surgery, and I never realized why I got a hard-on before surgery. For the longest time, I thought it was the surgery itself that was a turn on for me. And I was ever so grateful that I had gone into a profession that could give me so much pleasure in addition to paying me so well. But then I slowly caught on. I was aroused by the prep. The shaving and the cleaning off of the lather."

"I can show you a really good time without this, you know," I stuttered out. "I can give you a fuck like you've never had before." It was grabbing at straws. But I was worried about where this might lead. Whether he had even darker fetishes. I usually liked to be very sure of a client before I was tied up.

"Yes, yes, I'm sure—and perhaps you shall," Gordan said in a faraway voice, which told me that he was locked into his fetish. "You know, though, that after I knew what it was that I wanted, I had a dilemma. I couldn't really take the risk of pursuing this on a real patient. Besides the fact that the operating room is full of people in this stage, there where phenomenal risks with the patient's lawyers. So, you know—"

He had broken off because his mouth was full of foam and nipple now. He had shaved my chest, down to my navel and was cleaning up the lather with his tongue. He was really good at it, and I wondered how much practice he had had with this. How many before me? If other guys in my profession had gone missing, I think I would have known. The agency would have known. But, what if I were the first?

I was so deep in worry and thought that I didn't know how long it had been since he'd stopped tonguing me down. When I looked around, I saw that he already had his scrubs off and was putting his white lab coat back on over his naked body. For his mid fifties, he really looked good. But, at the same time, too good. Plastic. I bet he'd had every inch of his body done and redone. And I wondered if they really could enhance a penis like that with plastic surgery. His body was hairless, so at least he carried this fetish of his through to himself.

He opened a condom package and crowned his pride and joy. Time for something I was more familiar with.

Gordan moved to below me, and I felt the lower appendages of the operating table, the arms to which my legs were strapped, being widened and bent so that I was in what I imaged to be the "birthing" position, legs bent and my feet trapped flat-footed in stirrups on jointed steel appendages feeding off from the sides of the table. Gordan was standing between my legs, and I saw the gleam of the metal aerosol can caught in the glare of the overhead operating lights.

Cold, wet. My pubes were being lathered up. And then my asshole too. I tensed up as I felt one of his fingers breaching my rim and pushing into at least the knuckle, taking lather with it. I did my best to relax as I looked down and saw the razor hovering over my pubes.

I panted shallowly and tried to be professional and not whimper or beg as I felt the razor scraping across my groin. Gordan was fisting my cock with his other hand, holding it out of the way and stroking it up and down. I was involuntarily engorging.

Which was fine. He'd paid for the service, and I would give the service. If I was going to beef, it would be to whoever I could find in the agency above Leon, maybe Rex Reeson, the owner of the whole shebang—but after having tried me out that first time himself and deciding I was good enough for his stable, I hadn't seen much of him at all. It had been made clear that Leon ran his stable. And it would be no good to let Leon know I thought I had a beef about this assignment. If I ever got home from this assignment, of course. That would really amuse him, that would.

I watched Gordan's head come down to my groin and lick at the lather and then up the side of my cock, and he swallowed me and constricted his cheeks around my tool. I groaned and strung a series of appreciative-sounding yeses for him and started a shallow rhythm in my hips to let him know that his was a superior suck.

After a bit of this, he lifted off my cock but still held it in a fist as he lathered up my inner thighs and began to scrape and tongue again.

Then the razor wasn't scraping. The finger wasn't in my hole. I almost lifted up off the table as Gordan thrust his cock inside me, running thickly and deeply at the first thrust, his entry smoothened by the lather he'd shot up into me.

The shave was finished. He was fucking me in deep thrusts, fully aroused by his fetish, ready to finish off the surgical fantasy.

There was an intriguing rhythm to his fucking. He was gripping my knees with his hands, and as he pushed inside me, he spread my legs out wide to the side, and as he withdrew, he pulled them in to touch his waste. But periodically he changed the pattern, which made me gasp with surprise.

Other than the unusual rhythm, I well knew the ass fuck part of the ritual. I cried out for him, telling him how good he was and how I wanted it never to stop, and Gordan rode with it. Thrusting and thrusting and thrusting. Making animal noises, while I moaned and groaned and told him he was killing me but not to stop.

He was as good with his cock as he had been with his razor. And I was enjoying this part—but doing all I could to make him enjoy it too. Enjoy it far more than the shaving part and certainly far more than any part he might be planning to proceed to after this. I wanted him to want me to be giving him the best of times and wanting me back some other time. Not carrying on with any possible terminal plans in this session.

With an exclamation, Gordan pulled out of me, jerked off the condom and shot up over my balls onto my now-smooth groin.

I sighed deeply and collapsed back onto the paper sheeting, only then realizing that I had arched my back and had brought my buttocks off the surface of the table to meet him thrust for thrust in his wild, exuberant fucking.

I did everything I could do to act like what we had done was totally exhausting, if totally wonderful—for both of us—and that we had done what we were going to do. But then I looked up at the clock on the wall and realized that he had nearly two hours left on his contract. I groaned, and this time it didn't have anything to do with sex.

I refocused on Gordan. He was opening another condom packet. This time he rolled the condom onto my cock, which, conveniently, was standing at full attention and was hard as a rock. He let loose another cloud of lather on my capped tool.

Then, moving real well for his age, Gordan came up onto the operating table and knelt, straddling my hips, facing me. He held my cock rigid while he slowly encased my cock with his channel and began to slowly ride me. This was another maneuver I was adept at, so I lifted my hips off the surface of the operating table and gave him a good time and appropriate sounds of pleasure and, in the end, a good feel of the bulb of a condom billowing forth to capacity well up his canal.

I wondered if the clock had stopped. He still had more than an hour when we were done with that. He went back to the razor and the lather, and my legs and arms were completely denuded and exposed to the breezes.

We had come to what I thought of as the danger point, but Gordan's fetish turned out to have its limit. He released me from the table and started talking about how good I was and how he was pleased with the service.

This was when the customer service I was known for and that brought me return requests kicked in. Comfortable now that nothing threatening was going to happen, I turned to him and took his cheeks in my hands and gave him a big sloppy kiss on the lips. Our eyes were inches away from each other, and I watched him turn from surprise to pleased to renewed arousal.

"God, you're a superb cocksman," I whispered when we disengaged. "You have time left on the clock. Could you fuck me again, please?"

Flattered and delighted and immediately up to the challenge, he told me how much he'd like to do that in a flustered voice, and I turned and bent over onto the operating table on my now-hairless belly.

I felt the cool, wet lather at my asshole again, and then he was fucking me, slowly at first, and then in a frenzy, as I writhed under him and screamed out at the thick, deep taking. He covered my back with his torso and I turned my head and we kissed. He was trembling almost uncontrollably as he came again deep inside me.

I was whistling as I folded the extra thou into my billfold and settled into the BMW for the drive back down out of the Hollywood Hills. Leon wouldn't hear a whisper of complaint or description from me about this assignment. I knew that would drive him crazy.

Chapter 13: Beautiful Bondage

I had been told that the assignment was a bit kinky, but a weekend stopover in Hawaii and three days on my own in Tokyo, paid for by the generous fee addition, were enough for me not to care. My pimp, Leon, told me to make myself blond all over, which I had grown used to in any assignment sending me to the Orient. In fact, this request was made so much in general, that I was contemplating going blond permanently.

I was a bit intrigued by this assignment because I was told up front that the client was Matsu Shinjuto, an elusive Japanese billionaire, much of whose wealth came from his Japanese ink paintings and block prints of ancient Shinto shrines during the various seasons.

The limousine sent for me at the hotel stopped at a massive set of iron gates at the base of a sharp steep slope up a hill, heavy with ferns and carefully pruned weeping trees, and I climbed slowly up to a hilltop eerie high above Kyoto, where my client had placed his many-pavilioned Japanese-style mansion floating over Japan's cultural capital. As I climbed, I looked up at the red-lacquered railings on the terraces above, sensing many sets of eyes on me, assessing me, although I wasn't able to discern any movement.

I entered the compound through a brightly painted torii

gate, ushered by a black-robed figure nearly bent at the waist. We moved silently on stockinged feet through a series of white rice-papered-walled, wood-framed pavilions seemingly floating in the clouds. Between each pavilion was a austerely beautiful, uniquely landscaped stone garden atrium straight out of the master's style of painting. I was to find that his art went much beyond the scenic, however.

When I entered into the first courtyard, a deceptively small, square space that used stunted Japanese maples, mountain-like rock formations, and running water to provide the illusion of scenic splendor, I was escorted into a small room off to the side. I was asked by the elderly, severely demeanored gatekeeper who had taken over as my escort at the entry of the second pavilion, which seemed to mark the beginning of the core living area of the compound, to strip down and wrap an emerald-green kimono around my torso and tie it off with a royal-purple sash. There was a tube of scented lubricant on a low stool, with instructions, written on rice paper in elegant, black-inked calligraphy, to apply it generously to my channel. None of this was shocking to me, of course. I was way beyond the capability of being shocked in the world of the extremely highly paid male prostitute.

When I was escorted to the third pavilion, I was motioned to sit, yoga style, with my kimono billowing about me on a cushion placed in front of a squat rosewood tea table. Another, more luxurious and plumper pillow was set beside me. As a willowy young Japanese man in a shiny silver and black kimono served me a glass of perfectly chilled Sapporo beer, I gazed, in great interest and awe at the walls about me, where a large collection of traditional Japanese ink drawings were displayed—composed of highly graphic male-male gay erotica set in some ancient oriental era.

As a whole, the exquisitely drawn collection could stand as a tutorial in the many exotic positions men could get into in fucking each other. I was particularly drawn to the style termed Shinjuto—because they unmistakably were the work of the master—used to gain maximal erotic images from the clothing. Rarely were the models completely naked; rather, Shinjuto had

136

used clothing to help enhance the senses and understanding of the paintings. By exposing only fingers on a nipple and a half-buried cock in an ass peeking out of an opening of billowing kimono material—along with the expressions on the faces of both taker and taken, Shinjuto had perfectly caught privacy and sensuousness in one work. And in yet another, by showing the clothing in dishabille as in a struggle, the bent-over position on a moss-covered rock in a garden, and the panicked look in the face of the significantly smaller, taken one and of the flailing, helpless position of his arms, Shinjuto caught nonconsensual ravishment perfectly.

"Ah, do you find my private collection to your liking, Mr. Smith? I presume we can refer to you as Mr. Smith in our arrangement?" Shinjuto had arrived, on silent rattan sandals, while I had been absorbed in his artwork, and settled very close beside me in a sigh of satin and silk. He was in his early senior years, at least into his mid sixties, but he looked toned and handsome in his traditional kimono of pure white undergarments and an over dress in a blue oriental waves pattern. He was well groomed and had long, elegant, strong fingers that attracted the eye with their fluid motion and precise placement while he talked.

"Yes, that name will do, Sensei," I responded, using the term for master teacher and lowering my eyes as I had been instructed to do in a quick tutorial I had been given before I left Los Angeles. Shinjuto was paying top dollar, and I was warned to treat him as such. "And, yes. I find your art extraordinarily . . . melting. It has me . . . excited . . . with anticipation, if I might be so bold as to say."

I saw no reason to mince words. Shinjuto already had one hand behind me and at the nape of my neck, running his elegant fingers through my blond hair and his other hand buried inside the folds of my kimono below the purple sash and gently encircling my engorging cock. The preparation, the foreplay, had already begun.

"And which do you find most erotic, Mr. Smith? Perhaps that one over there, depicting much of what we are engaging in now?"

He had indicated the work where the two figures were nearly fully clothed but undoubtedly steeped in a very intimate act of taking. As he spoke, he had untied my sash and folded back the material at my breast, exposing one of my nipples. And his fist had brought my cock out from the folds of the material below where the sash had fallen away.

I sighed and trembled for him as I had been carefully taught men of refinement and an artistic temperament appreciated. The fingers at the nape of my neck tightened, as did the fist on my cock. Shinjuto pulled my head back and down, and I arched my back for him, my chest expanding and bulging out from the draped kimono.

"I wish you to come for me, Mr. Smith. In good time, while I tell you why I have engaged your services."

So, it wasn't to be just a simple fuck. What he was doing now wasn't the main thrust of why my time and body had been bought by him for top dollar. His lips and teeth went to one of my nipples as my back was arched by the tension of his closed fist in my hair and his other fist slowly and relentlessly jacked me off. He had a thumb on my piss slit, and as I flowed in precum, he thumbed the fluid around on my swollen glans.

"Yes, like that, Mr. Smith," he said when he lifted his head from one nipple in preparation for giving equal attention to the other one. "I want to see how large you can become. I was explicit about that . . . and it seems my desires were satisfied."

"I am paying well for you, Mr. Smith, as you no doubt are aware, but you are a means for me to make millions in your American dollars."

I moaned and trembled a bit at what Shinjuto was doing with his mouth and fist. He drew his head back and watched the effect of his artwork, as he briefly took his fist from my cock and then glided the palm of his hand up my torso, his moistened thumb, moistened by my own precum and raised outside the fold of my kimono, up to my mouth. He rimmed my lips with the moisture from his thumb and then pushed it past my lips, into my mouth, and I sucked on it.

While he was doing this, he was rearranging my body as

well from where we had been sitting, yoga style, very close beside each other. He had moved one of his thighs beneath one of mine, and he was twisting my torso to the side, the arm of the hand that had been in my hair now wrapped around my shoulder blade, his arm supporting my torso in its twisted, but still upright position, and with an elegant, long-fingered hand palmed across a nipple.

"Have you ever heard of the Japanese art of *Kinbaku-ji*, Mr. Smith? Translated as 'beautiful bondage?'"

"No, no, I . . . haven't," I managed in a gurgling tone, the thumb of his other hand still in my mouth, before I involuntarily groaned. Shinjuto had moved his face inside my draped kimono, forcing my arm over my head, and he was licking his way up the side of my chest, headed for my pit. He had also pushed his thigh farther under mine, lifting my hips up over into his lap. His kimono was open below his sash, and he was naked under the elegant white silk. His thighs were hard for a man his age, and I could feel the power of a strong cock, as well. I also could tell that it was sheathed, ready for me. There would be no clumsy pauses or wasted movement in his flow toward the taking of me.

"I have a Chinese client. A very, very wealthy Chinese client, Mr. Smith. He also has an attitude toward the West. He will pay me dearly for a collection of art, using the *Kinbaku-ji* style, but depicting the East dominating the West. You are to be my model for the West, Mr. Smith. And this client has eclectic tastes. While I am painting these scenes in traditional style, one of my students will be taking still and video photography, and my son will be developing a *Hentai* version." This has all been settled with your agency. There is no question of your obligation to participate.

I grunted and strained at this point, because the elderly Sensei, showing his extraordinary strength and flexibility and sorely testing mine, had drawn my leg straight up to rest on his shoulder between our torsos, which were now bowed away from each other. His thumb had left my mouth and had returned to fisting and slowly pumping my cock.

I could see this position mirrored in yet another of the

art works hanging nearby on his wall.

"Does that sound interesting to you, Mr. Smith?" Shinjuto asked this just before his teeth and tongue found the most tender hollow of my pit and started devouring me there.

"Yes. Oh, yes. Oh . . . OH . . . . YESSSS!" I cried out, not so much in response to his question, but because he had now opened and positioned my lubricated ass to his shaft, and he was burying his strong, virile cock deep inside me and somehow finding the leverage to piston fuck me as I found myself in a melting fuck position I'd never experience before. I knew it was a traditional position for Shinjuto, however, because, as I threw my head back in the passion of the taking by a Japanese master, my eyes caught yet another one of his drawings depicting exactly the same position.

* * * *

The modeling project was much more involved than I had thought it would be. After Shinjuto had jacked me off and cum with a very satisfied and decorous grunt, he rose and readjusted his kimono, which more or less fell back into an innocent drape line as he stood, and glided back out of the room. While a few young male attendants cleared away the pillows and table and half-empty glass of beer, which I could have used after the muscle-stretching exercise I had just gotten, a couple more helped me groan to my feet and took me to another pavilion, where I was bathed by them in a copper tub.

All of the male attendants were handsome young men. The two who attended me were especially nice, and apparently had been instructed to please me. Their appearance, along with remembering and reliving what Shinjuto had just so expertly done to me, made me hard again, and, seeing this and while they both giggled, one of the young men leaned over from above my head and possessed my lips fervently with me and reached over and pinched my nipples while the other lifted my hips to the surface of the water and sucked me to ejaculation.

After they had dried me off with warmed, fluffy towels and left me, I had a surprise visit from what must have been

Shinjuto's art students. I stood stock still and stark naked in the middle of the pavilion while four young men painted my body. What they were painting were depictions of Western arrogance and power projection—polluting mills, dollar bills, conquering armies, plundering ships, and every form of avarice and crass consumerism they could get on my body—in angry red and orange and yellow and black body paint colors. One design flowed into the next. My cock, of course, which they had to pump up to paint properly, was a guided missile. They were quick and inventive and highly skilled. I'm sure that they had worked all of the designing out in advance.

When I was "done," I was summoned to the first of several "stages." This was one of the austere stone gardens. The attendants made me recline on the center of a flattish platform rock, where I could barely touch the ground with the heels of my hands as they arched over and out at the corners of the rock toward the ground. White shiny silk runners of cloth ran out from under the rock, at the center of which, they must have crossed and been knotted, and streamed off at the four corners. I was forced to dig my heels into the sand at the lower quarters of the rock, and then the streamers were wound around my wrists and ankles, binding me on the surface of the rock to the ground in a backward crab position, my cock pointed at the sky.

Through intricate windings of the silken runners, my head was arched back with a strand running taut under my jaw, the runners criss-crossed my chest, and another of the strands wound up a leg and then under my balls and tightly encasing the root of my cock, which effectively kept my cock both pointed straight up and engorged.

Although I had sort of figured it out beforehand, I knew for sure what the body paint was about when I saw the two lithe but well-muscled and very agile Japanese young men who came out into the garden after I had, by the Sensei's definition, been "beautifully bound," or prepared for *Kinbaku-bi*. The two young Japanese were also covered in body painting— but in more subtle greens and blues and whites and certainly in more refined and artistic images than were slathered on my

141

body. Everything their bodies depicted was the antithesis of the crass and angry and grabby images on my body.

I got it. Shinjuto was going to be used as a traditional Japanese sexual art form to give his Chinese client exactly what he wanted—an exotic and erotic collection of art showing East controlling and fucking West.

And that's exactly what they did. After the master and three of his prized art students had arrived and settled themselves in three different areas of the periphery, the two young men representing the East began to regain the dignity of the East by putting it to the bound West. Shinjuto was sitting cross-legged, in an elegant heavily brocaded vermillion kimono behind a sketching easel. Beside him sat a younger man, of maybe nineteen or twenty, and achingly beautiful—but with a melancholy aspect. He handed implements and inks to the elder Shinjuto upon command, and, when not doing this, he was sketching with rice paper pad and charcoal. Every time I looked at him, I found him slack jawed and watching me intently. I knew he wanted me. But I equally knew that he wanted me to fuck him.

Another of the students was busily moving around the garden, snapping photos and switching now and then to video—and always checking and scowling at the light sources. The third young man, the one Shinjuto had identified as his son, was sitting as his computer, doing whatever one did to adapt what was happening in real life to the Hentai world.

But I hardly noticed the actions of either of the latter two; I had my mouth and ass full with the two painted models. I was sucking one off, my head pulled back by the "beautiful bondage" so that he could just pump his cock inside my mouth by standing above my head, his fingers busy worrying my nipples. And the other one was between my legs and fucking my ass, while his hand was moving my "missile" to lift off.

In a second "beautiful bondage" setting, I was lying on my back at the last step of a rock-based water cascade formation descending down into a small pond. My wrists and ankle were bound together by the silken runners, which then rose to the graceful limb of a pine branch jutting out over the water cascade. Two runners wound around my waist, with one snaked around an ankle of one of the painted East figures and then to the other, binding him to me, as he stood at the base of the cascade between my spread and raised arms and legs and fed his cock in my mouth. The other East model was lying below me in the shallow pond at where it was cascading down between my trussed appendages. Bondage runners ran from his waist up to around mine. His cock was buried in my ass, half visible and rocking in and out for the artists to see, appreciate, and capture in their various mediums.

In the third and last scenario, although it provided a double bonding image, I was taken into a large pavilion bedchamber. In the center was a large, square bed, covered in mussed silken sheeting of the purest white. Hanging from a hook in the ceiling above the center of the bed was a silken runner, the richest red this time, gathered up so that it was well off the bed. Similarly, there were two other hooks and red hanging runners at either side of the center hook, each positioned near the edge of the bed. I was forced down on my belly in the center of the silken sheets. My wrists were bound together behind my head and encircling my jawbone and then attached to a runner around my chest at the level of my pecs. Inside this runner clips had been sown into the fabric and were clipped securely onto my aureoles, pinching my nipples closely.

Another runner ran off of this chest wrapping from between my shoulder blades and went back and was tied to my left ankle taut enough to pull my leg at a side angle. A runner encircled my waist and another, wider-banded one tied at the chest banding both at the sternum and between the shoulder blades. It wound down and through my ass crack between these two points, winding once on each side around the waist wrapping as well. My right leg was bent back upon itself with a tight wrapping holding the ankle up against my thigh at an awkward position that, by design, left my butt cheeks stretched wide.

I didn't notice that the runner going between my crack had a shallow cylinder pouch in it at ass level until the East models began fucking me. They took turns. And although their

143

cocks weren't thick, they were long. The deeper they fucked, the deeper the pouch that now ran up inside my channel was pushed. And the deeper this was pushed, the more tension that was put on the "beautiful bindings" attaching at my chest and ultimately around my jaw and at my nipple clippings. With each thrust, my head was being jerked back, my back was arching involuntarily, and my nipples were being pulled.

From this point to the end, the photography guy was going to video only. He had his microphone down close to my head and he was capturing some sounds of taking like he'd never heard before.

Both I and the men below me on the bed were doing a lot of writhing, and the body paint was coming off onto the white silken sheets. While I was trying to focus on something other than this excruciatingly painful-pleasurable fucking, I briefly wondered how much Shinjuto could get for the framed silk sheet at an art auction in Chicago. Knowing that it could go for high money with the right background story, I was getting fully into this East fucking West scenario that had been created here.

The finale was a doozy. Before the two East models came this time, they untied my legs and undid the binding around my jaw, and I found out what the red runners on the ceiling hooks were for. The ones at the corner were let down and my legs were split wide and my ankles were bound in red well off the bed and straight out at my sides. The center streamer, which was on some sort of pulley system was lowered, and my bound wrists were bound on this and I was raised above the silken sheets in a spread-eagled form.

The two East models then laid stretched on their backs below me, their heads in opposite directions and joined at the pelvis, the thighs of one over the hips of the other. One of them held their two long, but happily not all that thick, cocks together until an attendant had wrapped a binding around the base of their cocks, making their tools one, thick cock. Then the binding between my ass cheeks was taken away, the pouch slurping out of my channel, as I was lowered onto the two cocks. Skewered deep by two throbbing, joined tools, and then raised, and lowered, raised, and lowered . . . until both of the East models had come in much jerking and thrusting up of themselves from below me.

* * * *

As I was being unbound and praised for my contribution to art by the attendants and the photographer, I looked up and saw Shinjuto standing there, half way between his easel and the bed. He stood tall and straight, but he was shaking. And I could tell how wound up he was and moved to a higher plane of desire by the expression on his face alone. His sash had come untied, and the kimono had fallen away from his body. His heavily muscled chest was heaving, his nipples were puffed and rock hard, and there was a thin film of sweat glistening at his sternum. His erection was gigantic and angry red and slightly bobbing up and down.

The young man who had been handing implements to him and crouching beside him and sketching as well was still huddled back at the easel. I could see the want and need in his eyes as well. But I could also see fear and confusion, and it hit me at that moment that he had no experience in this. Only want and need.

"Come. I am well pleased," Shinjuto said in a wavering, barely controlled voice. "I will pay double. I will also charge double. And my client will gladly pay it upon seeing the samples."

He took my hands, my wrists still bound in "beautiful bondage," in a firm grip and led me over to the side of the room. There was a contraption in front of the rice-paper wall that looked like the side view of gymnasts' parallel bars—quite widely divergent parallel bars. The lower bar was the nearer one and was set at mid-thigh level. The one beyond it was set at shoulder height. On this higher bar, there were silken strands wrapped near each end.

In short order, my thighs were straddled on the lower bar and my ankles were bound above the higher bar at the widely spread interval. Shinjuto was crouched down behind me, his angry red, gigantic tool working its way up into my ass channel, his long, elegant fingers digging into my aureoles. My bound wrists were thrust over his head, joined behind his neck, which held my shoulder blades against his heaving chest.

I saw the young assistant in my periphery vision, at Shinjuto's elbow.

"Please, uncle, please. You said that I might . . ."

"Yes, Kanto, you may have your first taste."

The younger Japanese came around in front of me and knelt and tentatively started to taste my cock. As he worked at it, he quickly got better, no doubt having had a lot of instruction in the theory of it from his father's art.

"One last *Kinbaku-bi*, just for my own pleasure," the Sensei was muttering. "This does not go to the Chinese client. I have this part of you for myself."

I was thinking—between grunts and groans at Shinjuto's expert fucking and the young one's pleasurably learning—that it was a shame that this wasn't being captured in art if it meant so much to Shinjuto.

But even as I thought that, the pavilion wall panels before my eyes were splitting and being drawn back . . . to reveal a life-sized, obviously Shinjuto master painting of just what I would see if there had been a mirror there. The agency must have sent him a photo of me, because it clearly was me in the painting, trussed up on this apparatus—and it clearly was Shinjuto fucking me and showing a pleasure in the fuck in his face that I couldn't see in real life from where I was bound. And between my legs in the painting was the bobbing head of the handsome young Japanese nephew of the master.

Shinjuto had orchestrated it all. He was the master.

* * * *

I never saw Shinjuto again. As far as he was concerned, I'd done what I had been paid handsomely to do and now he was going to be paid even more handsomely for having created art out of his sensuous, torturous taking. He was the master, the Sensei. Before he released me from his bondage, however, he told me that before I left Japan, I would received one more token of his appreciation. But that I should only accept it—and he declared that it would be quite valuable—if I would grant the one wish of the one who delivered it to me. I hesitated slightly in responding, but he reassured me that the present would be worth far more than I would have to give for it, so I told him I accepted.

I was intrigued about what this present might be, and it was that more than the declared value of the gift that made me say yes. Shinjuto had been very generous to me. But, despite all that I had made—and even how much I had enjoyed the exotic taking and learning of the Japanese sexual art of *Kinbaku-bi*, I was just too mischievous and imbued with the need to control in my heart to leave it all completely at Shinjuto's design and command.

I had seen that Shinjuto was holding his nephew back—that he had every intention of teaching him in the ways of men with men. But that he was going to dole it out piecemeal and almost reluctantly—and completely under his control and at his direction. That he was going to torture the handsome youth with it.

Kanto, the nephew, was in the pavilion where I was being cleaned up and given a chance to rest. I could tell that he wanted to linger when the others were finished, and I decided to help him with that and to assert a little control of my own and to leave my mark on Shinjuto's well-ordered and orchestrated life.

As Kanto was putting the towels into a bin, I went over to him, took him by the hand, and walked him around the walls of the pavilion, which was the same one in which Shinjuto had first taken me. We viewed the erotic art together, going from one to the other. I felt the intake of his breath and his tightening up as we stood in front of one that showed a young, willowy Japanese receiver rolled up onto his shoulders on a mat, his torso rising in the air and the older muscleman Japanese giver standing over him, one leg over the thigh of the younger one, whose heel rested on the older one's butt cheek, the older man holding the younger man's leg at the knee. The younger

147

man's other leg was spread out wide, being held by the older man's hand under the thigh. The muscleman Japanese was fucking down into the receiver's hole, his thick cock only half buried. The expression on the giver's face was one of triumph and lusting cruelty, and the younger receiver's head was arched back in a cry of passion and overstretching.

I unknotted the sash of my kimono and let it drape open. And I searched down in the folds to ensure that the tube of scented lubricant I had retrieved from the changing room earlier and hidden there was still there. Then I came up very close behind Kanto and drew him into me.

He shuddered at the feel of my cock in the small of his back, and he moved as if to pull away from me, but I held him fast to my chest. I held his torso to mine with a palm spread on his chest, and I untied his kimono with the other hand and, tugging at the kimono at his shoulders, made it drop unto the tatami mat below.

Kanto whimpered and struggled again, but I held him fast with a palm over his chest and the other hand going to his cock. He was already almost fully aroused. He was ready for me already.

He swiveled his head away from the painting, but I raised one hand to his jaw and held him there, face forward, fully looking at his uncle's masterwork of an older, muscled man dominating the younger virginal man. I got a large glob of lubricant on the fingers of the other hand, and I started working his tight asshole with my fingers. First one finger and then another.

Kanto was panting heavily and moaning, and I could feel his legs going to rubber. But I held him up with the framing hand under his jaw, forcing him to look at what was happening in the painting and with the strong finger of my other hand skewering up into his tight ass.

When I felt he was open enough to take me, I crouched down at the knees a bit and just picked him up off the floor with my hands on his waist and sat him down on the crown of my cock. He cried out at the pain of the taking, but now he had thrown his hands around my neck and locked his fists and his chest was arched out. He jutted his butt cheeks back into me, helping me to bottom.

We were united there, joined at the cock and channel for several long minutes, while we waited for his virginal channel to stretch to accommodate me and his pain and suffering to turn to wanting and lust. We were both panting, and he was groaning and moaning and telling me he never knew it could be like this and that this was his first time—which he hardly had to tell me.

Holding him to me with one arm across his panting chest as I lapped him in my semicrouched position in front of the painting, I reached down and fisted his cock in my other hand. He ejaculated almost at once with a joyous shouting that sent my own fluids spewing through me and deep into him.

Again we held the pose for several minutes as we cooled down and recovered the strength of our manhood, which he was able to do quickly because of his youth and because it was all so new and arousing to him—and I was able to do through professional conditioning.

Still, I had thought that would be enough. I had taken the virginity of Shinjuto's precious nephew, who he intended to slowly cultivate. I had thus accomplished my little flash of mischief and grabbing for control. And, just as important, I had thoroughly enjoyed myself.

That thought caught in my mind with a guilty twist, though, because Kanto was shaking inside my grasp. Perhaps I hadn't thought of him well enough in all of this. I'd thought he wanted to be relieved of his virginity as soon as possible, and his body had been sending out unmistakable signals to me. But he was trembling, so maybe I was wrong. Maybe he was upset at what he had lost.

"Kanto—" I started. Not really know how to say it; not even knowing what to say, what to ask. I couldn't given him back his innocence.

"I'm sorry. I can't pay you much," be blurted out, ending it with a sob. But then he continued in a flood. "I know you make a lot of money at this. I have very little, but I could send you a little at a time . . . for as long as it takes."

"Oh, Kanto," I said and then laughed with relief. "I didn't do this because I wanted you to pay me for it. I did this because I thought it was what you needed, and, frankly, because you are super hot and I wanted you. I don't have to be paid when I want to do it. You honor me by giving my your virginity. You don't know how thrilling that is to a man. To be the one to deflower a hot young man like you. So, now, shall we clean up and—"

"No. Please . . . no." His voice started off stubborn but then got shaky again.

"No, what?" I asked, surprised.

"The painting. Can you fuck me like they are doing in that painting there first?"

"Yes, of course," I said, laughing again. And, taking him off my lap and turning him around and setting him gently down onto his shoulder blades, I showed that I could . . . and I did.

* * * *

Three days later as I was packing my bag and getting ready to leave Tokyo after having had a great time in the Shinjuku ni-chome bar scene—and after bar hours activities, where I picked up some extra cash from several randy Japanese men with open and overflowing wallets, I answered a knock at the door. Shinjuto's son stood there, grinning in recognition and, no doubt in remembrance, and, after we both bended in synch low at the waist, handed me a wrapped package.

"From Sensei Shinjuto, with regards and thanks," he said. And then he came out of his bow and gave me "the look," and I then knew much of what receiving the gift would entail.

"My father said that you would grant me my one wish," he said, and then, when I nodded in assent, he said, "My one wish is one last Kinbaku-bi with you. I assure you that it will not be as strenuous for you as my father was."

"Certainly," I said. "Come in."

I was already starting to strip down when he went back

150

out in the corridor and returned with a laptop computer, which he sat at the foot of the bed, facing the headboard, and revved up. He also had red silk bindings with him.

I watched the computer screen in fascination as he put me into beautiful bondage, one wrist bound to the railing of the bed's headboard at the left corner and the other wrist and my left ankle loosely bound together at the right corner of the headboard. I was then trussed up, my butt resting on the side edge of the bed near the headboard, left leg raised and torso stretched back toward the other side of the bed.

What fascinated me with the computer display was that it was of an animated Hentai of the cartoon me and Shinjuto's son in just this position. Shinjuto's son stripped down. He was slender but well muscled, a handsome young man, and his quite presentable cock was already engorged. He must have been a little self-conscious about his endowments, though, or overly ambitious, because the cock on his Hentai character was the size of a baseball bat. But then, so was the dick on my Hentai character—and my character's hole was big enough to take the baseball bat.

I watched both on the screen and in real life, as Shinjuto's son bound his forearm to my right calf with the silken bounds. Then, already encased with a condom, he just pressed between my spread thighs and fucked me as closely as he could in real life to the exaggerated good sex unfolding in the Hentai animation on the computer.

When he was finished, he just quietly unbound me, turned off and closed his computer, gave me a look and salute of full satisfaction and appreciation, and departed.

When he was gone, I opened the package to find an ink drawing, done in bold strokes, undoubtedly by the master, Shinjuto—of me fucking his nephew, Kanto, in front of the painting depicting the same act.

I had to laugh. Shinjuto had mastered me again. He had planned even what I thought I was controlling—the deflowering of his nephew—for free. And he'd managed to get a free *Kinbaku-bi* fuck for his son thrown into the bargain as well.

Chapter 14: Suits

Leon, my pimp, was conducting warfare on me—denying me lucrative assignments to wear down my resistance to him. Whether or not this had been an intentional campaign from the beginning, I have no idea. But it was frustrating and was making me mad enough to lash out in some direction or other. The escort service had reeled me into an expensive lifestyle in L.A.—my own apartment, a BMW convertible I now considered a necessity, and fine clothes and club memberships—and now they were pulling it all away. Or Leon was. Each time I called to see if they had anything for me, Leon would start off by asking if I'd go with him to this or that, and I'd say no, and he'd say time were tough and they didn't have a hookup for me. Times weren't that tough. The type of man who came to this escort agency wasn't affected by a downturn in the economy—nor had he suddenly lost his desires and the fetishes that only an expensive operation like ours would cater to.

And I'd lost my dancing gig at Thunder Road too. I was sure Leon was behind that as well. I was a crowd favorite there and the place was doing good business. There was no real reason I'd be let off. I'd kept myself in tip-top shape. But doing that was expensive too. I was close to losing the apartment and the car—and the rest of the lifestyle I'd become accustomed to. And I wasn't a bit nearer to my real goal of breaking into movies than I'd been the day I put a foot into California.

The worst thing was that I was beginning to lose my enjoyment of having sex with men, of being dominated and learning what new and different fetish was out there I'd never imagined before. While I waited for assignments with the escort service, I'd taken two jobs at about the same level as every other guy trying to break into movies out here was doing. I was dancing at a B-level nightspot called Hernando's and was also car hopping at a swank hotel. Both kept the hook-ups with men coming, where the real money of such a job was. But the class of men wasn't anything like I'd grown to expect—and I was beginning to take my frustration and anger out on the johns, my last hope for continuing the good life. The bottom of this arc was probably the weekend I think of as the "night of the suits."

It was a steamy, smoke-filled night at Hernando's, and I and the other two guys had been dancing to the music on the small stage for twenty minutes. I was already down to the ten-gallon hat, the pinto pony hide vest, the cowboy boots, and the low-slung belt and six-gun holsters, with the even lower slung eight-inch gun swinging in between and nothing else on, when I felt the hand on the ankle of one of my boots.

The dude clinging to my boot looked cooler than a cucumber despite the heat and the indoor smog and even though he was wearing a suit—a finely tailored Brooks Brothers navy blue pinstripe silk suit that was cut close to his well-cut body. He looked like money all over. His pale blue dress shirt was as finely and closely cut to the perfect curves and bulges of his body as his suit was, and the gold studs in his shirt cuffs and his Rolex watch sparkled in beams from the strobing lights overhead. He was flashing a set of ultrawhite, perfectly capped teeth at me in a full-lipped, sensuous mouth. He also was flashing a fifty-dollar bill.

Having gotten my attention by grabbing my boot as I was undulating on the stage above him, stroking myself off, not far from giving the crowd the thrill it had come to see, he yelled up to me through the loud music and the din of cat calls and stale suggestions. "You fuck me? More of this if it's good for me."

Fifty dollars? His tie alone was worth four times that. An insult. I was having offers twice that high thrown at me by the plumbers and electricians sitting all around him. God, when I was getting top-level hookups through the escort service, I was making sixty times that for an hour of my time. I crouched down and shot my load across the nice lapels of his $800 Brooks Brothers suit, and then I went home that night and fucked my bass-voiced boyfriend of the week until he warbled soprano. And I did it for free.

Three nights later I was at my other evening job, the more humbling one, as a car hop at the Honeywell Hotel. They made me wear a monkey suit there; I much prefer my cowboy outfit at Hernando's. It had been air conditioned and I was watched when I wore that one. I liked being watched; I was built to be watched. Here at Honeywell I was invisible; just part of the service in getting into and out of the hotel in a jiff. But at least here I got to jockey Porsche Boxsters—at least as far as the parking lot over in the shadows beside and behind the hotel.

I was contemplating being invisible when a honey of a silver Maserati Quattroporte drove up to the entrance and out stepped . . . the suit from Hernando's. At least he was still noticing me. He picked up on who I was right off, and I was afraid he might take a swing at me for messing up his Brooks Brothers suit—but he didn't. He was all flashy smiles and knowing looks. And he had been slumming the other night. Tonight he was wearing a lustrous brown Armani suit, easily worth three times what the blue pinstripe the other night had been worth, and he had on an ochre silk shirt under that, a flashy silk tie, and diamond cufflinks. All just as expensively and closely cut as the suit of the other night was. The man was dripping money. It was almost like I could walk along behind him and pick up gold coins as he shot them out of his ass like a bunny with diarrhea.

Two hours later he reappeared through the hotel

155

entrance. Another one of the car hops reached for his ticket, but he held off from giving it to the guy and looked around until he spotted me. He walked over, flashing that big, "see what I've got and you don't" smile at me, and handed me the ticket. But he also had $200 in folded fifties in the hand holding the ticket, and he wouldn't let loose of either of those or my hand as he said in a husky whisper, "Shall we up the ante?"

I was going off duty then anyway. And two hundred bucks meant a lot to me just then, no matter how niggling it was compared to what I'd become accustomed to—obviously far more than it meant to him. When I drove the Maserati around, I didn't get out of the driver's seat; I just leaned over and flipped open the passenger seat door. This was a signal to him, a gauntlet, so to speak. If we were going to do this thing, I was going to do the driving. I liked the idea of the $200, but if he thought he was going to get off as cheaply as that, he was mistaken. Tonight was going to cost him a whole hell of a lot more than $200.

He got in the passenger side without hesitation, and I fisted the stick shift and he fisted my stick as I drove him into the parking lot and back to the corner where I had my boyfriend's Chevy van parked. My boyfriend was a bit adolescent, and he kept what he called a "love mobile." I'd taken it to work this evening because he wheedled the BMW out of me to try to impress a producer at a party he had been invited to.

I clicked open the sliding side door to the van, and the suit got in without hesitation and whistled in appreciation. The van had most certainly been outfitted for love. Smoked windows; floor, sides, and ceiling covered in padded sapphire blue velour; straps anchored strategically here and there, and an easily accessible sound system with speakers embedded all around. And that stool. He'd be introduced to the stool later.

I told him to take off his shoes in my home—just like they do in the Orient. And while he docilely did that, I climbed into the van, stripped off the hated car jockey's uniform, clicked the side door shut, and turned on the sound system. I selected Lebanese music with a good strong beat and a tortured-voice singer singing in a manner that would disguise most any yowling coming from inside the van. I planned on there being some yowling.

First thing I did was tie up the dude's right wrist to a strap in the ceiling of the van, a little behind the front seat. I didn't want him going anywhere or getting the notion he was going to be in charge. He hunched there, in his Armani suit, his free hand searching between my thighs.

I stripped the Rolex from his left wrist and, after entertaining him with how well balanced it was when I hung it on my hard cock and spun it around for him, I tossed it into one of his shoes. I didn't want the reminder of money ticking away while I worked here. Then I got his fist off my cock, where he had found the mushroom cap gold-studded ring I'd been tricked into having installed at a Prince Albert club shindig and that flashed in the overhead bulb just as brightly as his diamond cufflinks did. Then I strapped his left wrist up to the ceiling.

I unbelted and unzipped him and peeled the Armani trousers and Calvin Klein briefs off his legs. And I wasn't delicate about it. I heard a rip and so did he, but neither one of us showed that we cared. I was moving with determination, and he was already wide-eyed and giving little panting sounds and murmured moanings. He had seen my eight inches in full erection already. He knew what I was packing for him.

He was crouched there on his knees now, panting, in fine silk socks held up with braces under his knees and above his well-muscled calves, but still fully decked out in suit coat, shirt, and tie. I crouched between his spread knees, letting my cock snake up under the tail of his shirt and bedevil his navel while our lips were heavily engaged in a sloppy kiss. I unbuttoned the two middle buttons of his shirt, just enough so that I could spread the expensive, rustling silk and expose a puffed up nipple. Then I lowered my head and pushed his tie aside with my chin and worked his nipple through the opening of his shirt with my tongue and teeth.

He was moaning for me. Begging to be fucked.

157

I raised his legs, one at a time, and tied them to straps in the ceiling toward the back of the van. He was trussed up now and hanging like a deer over a campfire, face up to the ceiling. I threw a leg over his belly and put my hands on the back of the front seat on either side of his head and clicked my cock stud against his white teeth until he opened for me and gave me head. He gave me good head, moaning and groaning all of the time at the length and width and hardness of me. This is what he was paying for. This is what he was going to get.

When I was bored with this, I pulled my cock out of his mouth and threw my leg back over him. He watched in eye-slitted lust and interest as I opened a side glove compartment and took out a handful of condom packets. I opened a packet and rolled a condom onto my cock. Then I extracted a leather-studded cock ring and wrapped that around the base of my cock. The last item I pulled out of the compartment was a small bottle of KY. All the time he was whimpering for me, begging for me to get inside him.

He did look a little concerned then, though, when I reached up and undid the cuffs on his shirt on both sides and extracted his diamond cufflinks and then tied them with string to my cock ring. I was chuckling about him getting his money's worth out of this fuck. But he didn't seem all that amused.

He probably thought I was going to take my time and open him up real well for the fuck. But he was wrong there. I soaked down my cock with the KY and squirted enough into his hole for it to be beneficial for me. But then I was rimming him with my bulbous mushroom cap and pressuring his hole and making little forced entries and pulling back a little and then worrying the tight, unready hole again. And then, when I'd gotten the cap all the way in, I just thrust in and bottomed with one lunge. He yowled to the velour ceiling, hitting a high A even stronger and truer than the Lebanese musician was doing on the background music. And he continued to yowl, first in pain and then in consuming desire, as I picked up the beat of the music and fucked him and fucked and fucked him.

As I fucked him, I bunched up that silk ochre-colored shirt of his in my fists and literally ripped it off his body,

158

pulling the shreds of it from underneath his tie and the brown Armani suit coat. The dude didn't seem to care; he was swinging his body against my plunging cock with the beat of the music and warbling right along with the Lebanese singer. He came in great spoutings long before I did.

Sometime during the fucking, I felt the diamond cufflinks come loose and work themselves up the dude's passage with the thrustings of my cock. The dude gave little yipping sounds at this added fiber to his ass's diet, but he made no objection. He wasn't objecting to anything now except to the possibility that I might stop stroking his ass. I almost went on a laughing jag mid fuck at the image of how he'd be shitting diamonds for the next day or so. Thinking about that being close to the meaning of being filthy rich.

When I was spent, I leaned into him and encircled his torso with my arms and felt the fast beating of his heart next to mine through the shredded ochre silk until he had calmed down and I had started to reload. He was sighing and whispering endearments to me, telling me how good I was and hoping I wasn't finished taking him.

I wasn't finished. Not by a long shot. This wasn't nearly expensive enough of a fuck for this dude yet.

I released both his legs and arms, but I immediately turned him and reattached his wrists to straps at the base of the front seat on either side. He didn't object. He was licking his lips. I was giving him exactly what he was seeking from me. I pulled over a low, velour-covered stool with a hole in the seat and forced the dude down on top of it on his lower belly. His cock and balls were poked through the hole and he found that he was encased in a sleeve around his cock and sacks around his balls, which were the business end of a cock milking machine. I strapped his hips to the stool so he couldn't extract his cock and then turned on the machine. The machine started to slowly contract the sleeve around his cock and undulate over it, teasing his cock to engorge and discharge. And the sacks around his balls also contracted and squeezed in a fascinating rhythm. He seemed to like this, and began moaning almost immediately. He'd maybe have second thoughts after he'd shot off the first time and found the machine wasn't satisfied with that.

I crouched up where he could see me and changed the spent condom for a fresh one and lathered it down with KY. And then I was behind him, making him push his knees wide, his butt waving in the air. I straddled him, my thighs on either side of his waist, above his stretched thighs, my hands on his shoulder blades. And then I reared my hips back and thrust my sheathed cock inside him and pumped hard and fast.

He was singing a loud duet again with the Lebanese singer to the heavy beat of the music.

I tore the coat off his back while I was fucking him and the stool was milking him, and I put it in front of his face and tore the lining out. He didn't care. He was going over the moon with what I and the stool were doing to him. I pulled the expensive silk necktie around his neck to his back and used it as reins as I did a bull bucking rodeo exhibit on his buttocks. I could feel the diamond cufflinks churning around inside him and he could too. I could tell that by the screams of passion he was making. The Lebanese singer was reaching a climax in his yowling and so were the dude and I. The dude shuddered and came, and then moaned as he discovered that the stool wasn't finished with him. And then I gave a cowboy whoop and came as well.

After a second and then a third ride, and continuous attention from the stool, I was finished with him. I turned off the stool and untied him and he just huddled there in thank-you whimpers. As a parting gesture, I untied his necktie, rolled the spent condom off my dick, and wiped my dick and then his asshole with the silk tie and stuffed it in his mouth. His gaze told me that he was still in love. It didn't seem like anything I was going to do was going to tell this guy where he could stuff all his money, as far as I was concerned. Still, I figured when the semen had drained out of his eyes, he'd come to his senses and survey the damage I had done to all his expensive stuff and get a little mad.

I put my car jockey duds back on and made sure he could see where I was leaving the keys to his Maserati. And then I left him there, in the back of the Chevy van, and walked back over to the entrance of the hotel. Within minutes a studly black guy gave me a ticket and a look, and, when I'd driven around his shiny black Mercedes CLS55 AMG, we were driving off to his up-town penthouse apartment, where I fucked him silly and he fed me breakfast, begged for and received my bone a second time, and then brought me back to the hotel for the now-deserted Chevy van.

Two days later, I was dancing on the stage of Hernando's when I felt a fist wrap around the ankle of my boot. There, gazing up at me with love-struck eyes was the suit, now outfitted in a black sharkskin $3,000-plus Valentino, diamond cufflinks cleaned and polished and gleaming in beams from the overhead strobe lights—holding a wad of hundred-dollar bills in his other fist. Wanting me again.

I knew then and there that I needed to get out of this business. The men weren't going to make that decision for me. They were always going to come back for more. And my anger was mounting to where something was going to have to happen or I'd explode and do something I'd regret for the rest of my life.

Chapter 15: Rebalancing

The rent was due, the car payment was due, I'd torn my best gabardine trousers. The notice attached to my locker at the swim and tennis club that I'd have to pay my bill or clear out my locker was the clincher. Either my pimp, Leon, had won in his campaign for me to knuckle under to him or I might as well use the last money in account for a one-way ticket back to North Carolina. In the end, if this was the end, I was winding up like 99 percent of all of the other young hopefuls who came out to the West Coast to break into movies—back home taking credit cards at the gas station checkout registers.

But this wasn't going to be the end for me, and I wasn't like nearly all of the other young hopefuls. I could be realistic. I would use what I had; do what I needed to do.

I stood, naked in front of my mirror, and I decided that there was still some use left in this body—that this was a realistic assessment. When all of those other failed hopefuls were boarding buses back to Podunk, that would just mean that much less competition for me.

Most important, I reasoned, as I stood there and ran my hands over my hard-muscled body, I still enjoyed it—the sex. The sex with rich and powerful men, each with a new and different fetish, but all having one thing in common—wanting me, wanting to release their desires and lust on and inside me. When it was no longer enjoyable . . .

I felt strong but trembling hands on my hips. I looked up in the mirror in surprise and just managed to recognize my former roommate and my mentor in the escort service, Zane, before his lips were buried in the hollow of my neck. He was standing behind me, already naked. I hadn't heard the click of my apartment door, and I hadn't seen Zane for weeks. We were supposed to play tennis at the club today, but when I'd seen the eviction notice there, I had left immediately in embarrassment.

He was close behind me, one hand having gone to one of my nipples and the other to my cock. I could already feel the want in him at the small of my back.

"I saw the note at the club," he murmured. "I paid your bill. We can still play our match."

"Perhaps a tennis match after one right here," I answered, relief flooding back into me. Leon had not been playing games with Zane as he had been with me. Zane was still getting high-priced hook-ups from the escort service. He could afford my club bill. More important, he was willing to pay for me. A much-desired escort himself and he was still willing to pay for me. I didn't have to look in the mirror for answers. Zane gave me the answer. I still had "it."

No, it wasn't time for me to give up yet.

"I want you. I want you now," Zane muttered hoarsely.

"Yes," I whispered.

"And not just for paying your bill."

"No, I understand." I responded.

He pulled me over to the bed and pushed me down on my side. He lifted my leg with one hand and was already thumbing into me with the other as I stretched out, opened the bedside table drawer, and retrieved a condom and the KY. Standing close behind me, raising my leg to his shoulder with one hand, he entered me strongly and immediately started stroking me hard sideways as I lifted my hands to the rungs of the headboard and hung on for dear life.

* * * *

The first step I took in my resurgence plan was to swallow my pride and call Leon. He was delighted to hear from me, thought it was great that I was interested in coming over for a swim, and assured me that right after our "swim," he'd have a good assignment for me that had just come in with my name "written all over it."

Leon was a cruel sex partner; I refuse to use the word "lover" in conjunction with him. It might have been largely my fault for having frustrated his advances for the better part of a year. But I somehow believe it was just his nature and that he would have been cruel in his domination no matter when I had given in to him.

And I knew how bad very shortly after I arrived at the Hollywood Hills home of Rex Reeson, the man behind the escort service. Leon, who was Reeson's factotum on the West Coast, had an apartment in Reeson's hillside mansion, so going to see Leon at home was the same as going to see Reeson.

When I arrived and walked around to the terrace, Reeson was playing the "meat" of a French bread sandwich on a lounger next to the pool. The two young French studs he'd brought home from Cannes eight months previously were still with him—or, rather, his cock was buried in one who was laying back on the lounger, and the cock of the other Frenchie was inside Reeson, as he crouched behind Reeson on the lounger and plunged into his ass each time Reeson pulled from the ass of the other guy to prepare to plunge again.

Leon wasn't there. Reeson seemed a little too busy to give an explanation and I'd never figured out if the French studs spoke any English at all. I stood next to another lounger for a couple of minutes and then shrugged and stripped down to my Speedo and took a couple of steps toward the edge of the pool. The day was hot and the pool looked inviting.

"You know . . . the rules," Reeson bellowed at me between huffs.

Oh, yeah, no clothes of any sort in Reeson's pool.

"Where's Leon," I asked. "I was supposed to meet him

here." I figured since Reeson knew I was here, there was no reason his fucking should get in the way of conversation.

"Got . . . tired of waiting. He'll be back. Took a cotton to the new pool boy. Oh, god, I think I'm gonna . . ."

I tuned him out—he was no longer paying a bit of attention to me anyway—stripped off the Speedo, and dove into the pool. I splashed around a bit, but slowly the unexpected sound started to creep into my consciousness and I glided over to the side of the pool near Reeson's lounger and rested my arms and chin on the side of the pool. The sounds didn't seem to be coming from poolside. Reeson was stretched out on the lounger on his back now and the French twins were tonguing him down. He was mewing. That wasn't the sort of sound that was assaulting my ears at all.

The sounds undeniably were those of a man being taken roughly.

"Where's that sound coming from?" I asked.

"The basement, through those speakers over there," Reeson answered in a small, faraway, fully satisfied voice. "That's the new pool boy. The speakers were set up for you. But Leon thought it would be better if you got to hear them in use first."

I knew for sure then it was going to be a tough journey getting back into Leon's good graces.

* * * *

I was determined to write my first taking by Leon off as just another different experience with an important client. I was equally determined not to scream in the taking as the pool boy did while I was poolside. I certainly was able to chalk up the first; I most certainly didn't accomplish the second.

Rex Reeson's basement was set like a BDSM movie set. Evidently anxious to consummate his victory, Leon took me first in an introductory fuck that wasn't too wild. I was bent over a padded bar, and he fucked me from behind while he slapped my butt cheeks red with the palms of his hands and did a little riding crop work on them. But then, in short order, he had me suspended on my back in a swinging sling with a black leather seat and velvet cuffs up the chain-link supports that trapped and spread wide my legs and arms when they were secure.

"Normally, I'd gag you," Leon said with a sneer. "But as I think you have figured out, I promised Rex that he could hear you. Don't worry, he also told me not to ruin you; you're still our best asset if and when you decide to play nice."

I endured the expanding cock enhancer pretty stoically—at least until near the end. Leon fucked me with an enhancer on his cock that spread apart, stretching the walls of my channel, as he pumped on a bulb attached to it by a long black tube. By the time he'd moved to the electric nodes on his cock as he pumped me, I decided the best means to get this stopped was to go with what he wanted out of me, and I opened my mouth and screamed to the blacked, stone-walled corners of the chamber, my cries, I'm sure, resounding over the pool terrace as well.

This subjugation to the will of Leon did gain me a string of lucrative assignments that put me back into the financial black and shut up all of my creditors. Before giving me each assignment, Leon fucked me. But he never again was as cruel as that first time. Still, there was nothing about his taking of me that I found enjoyable. And it was from that time that I began to think about the possibility of giving up this life. I'd done little toward my larger goal of breaking into the movies beyond making some "maybe" connections to "maybe" influential people or beyond taking some courses that increased my grooming, presentation, and customer service skills. I'd found what I needed of this in a hotel management course of study. But I found myself thinking about what the possibilities were for my life beyond what I was doing now.

And that's when Howard came back into my life.

* * * *

"The Client asked for you specifically," Leon said over the phone. "And he's willing to pay top dollar. The name he gave was Howard Stidwell. He wasn't in our files, but the check he sent cleared and was quite enough to open our lists to him. Have you been moonlighting at our client level, Brian?"

"No, I don't think I've ever heard that name, Leon," I answered. "Maybe a pseudonym of some sort. Do I get the assignment or not?" I was a little antsy. The rent was just about due again.

I got the assignment and was directed to a marina down on the ocean. The man who met me at the side of a humongous, brilliant-white yacht was quite presentable. He was Hispanic and I'd never seen him before in my life, as far as I could discern. He was a muscle hunk, maybe in his late thirties and all decked out in sparkling whites.

"Mr. Stidwell?" I asked as I approached.

"You must be Mr. Smith," the man responded as he flashed me a big, gleaming-toothed smile. "Just a minute, please." He disappeared under the awning over the fantail of the boat briefly and then came back and ushered me on board.

"Please strip down and sit over there on the fantail bench," he said in an even, polite voice that made it sound as if he gave such an instruction on a daily basis—and for all I knew, he did. "I'll be back in a moment. We're casting off and I have to go forward to see us through the harbor."

I dutifully stripped and stretched out on the velour cushions at the bow of the yacht and under the shade of the awning as the ship started to glide out of the harbor. A shift in the curtains in the main cabin caused me to look in that direction, but they fell back into place before I could determine if anyone was there, looking at me.

As we reached the ocean, the Hispanic man came back to me. He was naked now and was in magnificent shape. As he reached me, he came down onto the bench seat with his knees, encasing my thighs between his knees and presenting his thick, half-hard cock for me to suck, which I did as skillfully as I had been taught.

After he was fully in the mood, he rose and sank down between my thighs, spreading them wide, and then sucked on my cock as his fingers he'd lubricated from a nearby bottle of

KY began opening up my channel for presentation to his prodigious cock.

He fucked me at long length and masterfully with his knees between my thighs as I lay back on the bench, my butt cheeks resting on his strong thighs. There was no kissing or other show of affection. All of his efforts were centered on his cock and on getting it as deep inside me as possible and in making me groan and moan at his stretching and deep possession, which I did with little need for acting.

Looking over his shoulder, I saw that the curtain in the main saloon was now fully open and that we were being watched. I wasn't left to wonder about this for very long. Shortly after I'd noticed the voyeur, the door to the cabin opened and a man emerged.

It all clicked into place. I now remembered who Howard Stidwell was. The resort hotel owner back on the Atlantic coast—the one who liked to watch me being fucked by his boat crew before taking me himself. Well, that was OK with me; let the games begin in earnest.

I grasped the Hispanic crew member's shoulder blades and pulled his chest into my face, where I bit gingerly onto one of his nipples while I set my hips churning against him, pounding back at him as hard as he was fucking into me. The Hispanic gave a little cry of surprise and lust and lost his composure, going at me like a jackhammer.

In short order the appetizer course was over, and Stidwell had taken me into the main cabin, had me stretched out on my belly on a large bed, and, saddled on my hips, was fucking me with all of his might.

"I don't suppose you believe this is a coincidence," he whispered in my ear when he was spent and lying full length on top of me, the two of us still one unit hinged together by his softening cock buried deep inside me. His hands had taken mine, our fingers entwined together, which told me all I needed to know about how much he wanted me.

I murmured my pleasure and that I was listening to him, not wanting to break the spell of the moment.

"I've been looking for you for months. That director

friend of yours, Martin Blixen, is a real bastard, but I was finally able to buy the information from him on where he'd sent you. I shouldn't have ever let you go. I want you back."

Where my life went to from that point was mostly thanks to Leon, I think, so I really should thank him and send him a hefty check, wherever he wound up. He had pushed me over the edge of enjoying the male hooker world.

I returned to Virginia with Howard, and he let me help run his resort hotel. The courses I had taken in California, not really knowing that I had already decided another direction for my life, helped me in successfully taking up my duties in the resort world. Howard even encouraged me to add a dinner theater feature to the resort, which fully satisfied my urge to be part of the acting life and which, not incidentally, was successful enough to rival the Barter Theater in southern Virginia in reputation. I never, ever invited Martin Blixen to direct there, however, although my first lover, Hunter Elliott, appeared regularly on our play bills.

Hunter also appeared regularly in Howard's and my bedroom, performing magnificently between my thighs as Howard watched in appreciation, working himself up to fuck me himself afterward.

When Howard died, he left the resort hotel empire to me, and I know he still watches and smiles down on me as I entertain all of the men I invite to my bed—having managed to leave "the life" before I stopped thoroughly enjoying having sex.

About the Author

Habu is one of the pen names of a former supersonic spy jet pilot, intelligence agent, male model, movie actor, and diplomat. A wild youth in South East Asia was spent enjoying whatever sexual opportunities came his way, and much of his gay male writing is about recalling incidents from those days and inventing ones he'd perhaps have liked to experience. He now leads a very quiet and ordinary happily married family life.

An American, he is a published mainstream novelist and short story writer under another name and in another dimension of his life. He has written or cowritten (with Sabb) over 500 published short stories and nearly 100 published erotica e-books, primarily of gay fiction but also memoir, straight fiction and ménage fiction. His hand and creative writing can be seen in stories and books by habu, sr71plt, Dirk Hessian, Shabbu, and Stephen Kessel—among unrevealed others that might surprise readers. The fictionalized GM memoir *Flying High, Diving Deep* is loosely based on his life experiences. He can be found at the adults only gay male site http://www.barbarianspy.com/, which he shares with Sabb.

BarbarianSpy

FOR LITERARY HEAT

Not all books listed below may currently be on release.

BOOKS BY DIRK HESSIAN

The Beautiful Way
Blue and Gray
Colonel's Treasure
Beginning of Time
Prophecy of Noto
The King's Men
Labyrinth

BOOKS BY HABU

Dark Angel Sounding
Across the Threshold
Cruising Through History
Flying High, Diving Deep
Hard Knocks U
Man's Man
My Neighbor's Hot Tub
Trip Money
Tropical Sizzlers
Vortex
The Indian Doctor
Luther
Clint Folsom Mysteries Compendium Volume 1
Clint Folsom Mysteries Compendium Volume 2
Grab Bag 1
Grab Bag 2
The Indian Prince
13 Ways for Halloween
Sailorboy
The Handyman

Home to Fire Island
The Sporting Life
Platres Conclave
Cairo Surrender
Fetish Galore!
Homeward Bound
Journey to Mirage
Choke Hold

BOOKS BY SHABBU

Yap, Yap
Dirty Pool
Operation Black Jade
Yap, Yap
Cigars!
Angel in the Barn
Gayly Complicated
Despoiling David
The Tree of Idleness
I Met a Man
The Interview
Rough Road to Happiness

BOOKS BY SABB

The Legend of Holleystone Grange
Surprise Encounters
She is He
Wrong Man
Loyal to his King
Barbarian Tales - Book One - Traveler's Tales
Barbarian Tales - Book Two - Journeys Begin
Barbarian Tales - Book Three - The Inheritance
Barbarian Tales - Book Four - Road to Persepolis

~